NO MOON NO STARS

GEORGE ROBERTS MCGILL

First published 2024

001

Copyright © George McGill 2024

The moral right of the author has been asserted.

To the men, woman and children
who lived, worked and died on the British coalfields.

Deep down the mine, three thousand feet,
In suffocating dark they died;
Above, the air stretched cool and sweet
League upon league – to them, denied.

No light illuminated their dark night,
No moon, no stars, but scorching breath
Of fearful fires in fearsome flight
Swept them to ravenous death.

Oh! God, whose awful power has hid
The warmth of summer suns in coal,
And man must delve and toil amid
Such dangers and let Death take toll.

Look down on them where'er they lie,
Who gave their lives for daily bread,
And then let Thine all-pitying eye
Rest upon us, uncomforted.

And pity us, whose strongest will
Is weak to pay so high a price
For warmth, for livelihood, and still
Stand helpless at the sacrifice!

Author's Note

No Moon No Stars is a story in a theatre script format commemorating the life and times of a coal mining family at the time of the Gresford Colliery Disaster, September 1934

CHARACTERS

MRS. JONES   40's, stern, not given to frivolity.

MR. ALBERT JONES   Her husband, tolerant, comic, coal miner.

DAVID   Their son, 14-15 years old, clever, naïve, technical.

RUTH (SHINO)   Their daughter, 5-14.

ARTHUR JONES   Widower/bachelor, coal miner, Albert's brother.

TAID (GRANDFATHER)   An old man, the Jones's lodger, suffering from dementia.

MRS MORGAN THE MILK   Delivers milk, busybody know-all.

JOHN HOPKIN   Boy/teenager next door. Mischievous, 16, coal miner.

MRS AND MR HOPKIN NEXT DOOR   Problem Family

JENNY HOPKIN   Girl next door (Quiet teenager.)

POLICE SERGEANT   Over 50

POLICE CONSTABLE   20s

REVEREND GOWER-JENKINS

MR JACOBS   Jewish tailor

BILLY WILLIAMS   Rogue

VARIOUS MINERS, DEMOLITION WORKERS, FRIENDS

SIR HENRY WALKER   Chief Inspector of Mines

NO MOON NO STARS

Musical Introduction

MENDELSSOHN: A MIDSUMMER NIGHT'S DREAM OVERTURE

ROBERT SCHUMANN TRAUMERFREI (DREAMING) from KINDERZENEN OP15

DEBUSSY: AU CLAIR DE LUNE

BEETHOVEN: MOONLIGHT SONATA

MOZART: EINE KLEINE NACHTMUSIK 1ST MOVEMENT EKN K525 LAST MOVE.

SIWSANN GEORGE: KEEP YOUR HANDS UPON YOUR WAGES. TRAD SONGS OF WALES Saydisc CSDL 406

BEETHOVEN: FUR ELISE

ELGAR: WHERE CORALS LIE

THE CARIOCA SONG from the film *Flying Down to Rio*

ACT 1

SCENE 1

ACT I

The stage is in darkness. The sound of the BBC broadcast is heard reporting the disaster at Gresford colliery. It fades into silence after the first few sentences. A spotlight focuses on an elderly man sitting in an armchair. (stage left/right). A care worker speaks to the man, and exits.

22nd September1934 BBC Radio news broadcast:

... rather cool in the north and north-west, but elsewhere the temperature will be about average. Outlook for Monday, rather unsettled. Copyright Reserved. The whole of today's news is overshadowed and darkened by a terrible mining disaster in North Wales. There was an explosion followed by fire at Gresford colliery near Wrexham early this morning. Of the men working in the mine at the time, more than two hundred safely reached the surface, but for the rest we deeply regret to say the position is extremely serious. Six bodies were brought to the top within a few hours of the outbreak. The Ministry of Mines has been informed that the number of men still trapped by fire in the pit is believed to be between a hundred and a hundred and twenty but it is improbable that full details will be known before tomorrow. Good progress is being made in subduing the fire and the rescue work is being vigorously continued in the hope of getting to the area where the men are cut off but the work is tragically difficult and already three men of the rescue party have lost their lives. We would like to express on behalf of our listeners our profoundest... etc etc etc

DAVID
Fifty years have now passed since the great disaster at Gresford Colliery which killed over two hundred and fifty of my friends and workmates. On first news of the explosion, there was hope of men still being alive underground, trapped by falls of rock, and waiting the rescue that was sure to come, but we soon realised that there was no hope and no rescue and that many of our loved ones were gone forever from us. The first I knew of something terrible happening was when my mother woke me up on Saturday morning at about quarter past two, and the continual sounding of the hooter at Gresford confirmed that it was indeed something very terrible. The remembrance of that doleful noise has stayed with me ever since. Since that terrible morning, my mind has taken me back a hundred times to the roadway that runs from the pit bottom towards the Dennis Deep along which Dad and me walked together so many times to our places of work. And I often think of our old house, what the better class of people would have called a humble workman's cottage, and indeed I did envy the boys and girls who lived in the big houses in the nice part of town, but I realised too late that our house and hearth was just as happy in its own way as theirs.

(MUSIC FADES FROM FIRST PART OF 1ST MOVEMENT OF BEETHOVEN'S MOONLIGHT SONATA.)

(A back kitchen in a small, terraced house. A stormy night with the sound of rain battering against the window. MR JONES is sitting in front of the fire reading a newspaper, The News of the World. TAID is asleep in the chair. There is a bucket catching drips of rainwater falling from the ceiling by TAID'S chair.)(Brightly lit)

MRS JONES *(At the front door.)* David! Davy! *(She slams the front door, enters the kitchen and slams the door behind her. She shakes her umbrella and Mr Jones hides behind his newspaper. She is wearing her best coat and hat. A gust of smoke rises from the fireplace every time the door is opened and closed.)*
Where has he got to, he knows it's the Vestry meeting tonight. It won't be worth going if he isn't here soon!

(She walks over to the back door and opens it, a gust of smoke blows out of the fireplace)

Davy! Davy! *(Shouting even louder. She leaves the back door open and comes centre stage)*
I've been everywhere looking for him, by the bridge, down by the railway, along Top Road, I nearly fell over walking down Rocky Road, if anyone had seen me they would have thought I was drunk!

MR JONES
Well there has been talk in the village!

MRS JONES
Oh shut up you fool!

MR JONES *(impatiently)*
Oh sit down and stop fussing!

MRS JONES *(sharply)*
He said he'd be back early! And he hasn't got a coat on, he'll be soaked.

MR JONES
A bit of rain won't harm him.

MRS JONES
A bit of rain indeed, I've never seen rain like it, he'll catch the influenza!

MR JONES *(even more agitated)*
Oh, goodness me!

MRS JONES It's not so long ago people were dying from the influenza and in this street and all. Look what happened to Mrs Davies's girl.

MR JONES
Will you close that door, woman!

MRS JONES (*goes to the back door*)
Davy! David! I bet he's with that John Hopkin again, I told him to keep away from him, he's no good!

MR JONES
But he only lives next door! What can he do, walk straight past him as if he's invisible? You can't expect Davy to ignore him, it's impossible. He's bound to want to knock around with the lad.

MRS JONES
Not if I've told him not to!

(*More smoke from the fire envelops Mr Jones*)

MR JONES
Will you close that bloody door woman! I'm getting smoked like a kipper here.

MRS JONES (*stands rigidly and stares at Mr Jones*)
Don't …. swear! Anyway, you was black when you came in and you haven't had a wash yet. (*His hands and face black with coal dust. He grumbles and washes in the sink*)

RUTH (*There is the rattle of a passing goods train. Ruth hides under the table. She has been sitting quietly in the corner*)
I don't like thunder Mama.

MRS JONES (*sympathetically*)
That's not thunder, SHINO, it's just a train passing over the bridge. Come here. (*Mrs Jones holds the little girl.*) You said he'd fix that broken slate, a fine job he made of it! Oh! When are we going to leave this place? You said we'd be gone by the New Year but we're still here, so much for your pal on the housing committee. Oh! That bucket's full, you'll have to empty it.

(*Water pours through the kitchen ceiling onto Taid who is sleeping in an armchair with his back to the audience. He jumps up, startled.*)

TAID
Iesu Mawr, what's happened!

MR JONES (*moves to the bottom of the stairs so as to collect upstairs bucket*)
Oh the bucket upstairs must have overflowed. A little bit of water, that's all, Dad.
(*He helps him back to his chair*) Don't worry, dad, it's not The Flood! (*Sarcastically.*)
There's a slate off the roof. (*Goes upstairs.*)

11

(*The door opens, Davy enters, soaking wet*)

MR JONES
Where have you been? Your mother's hopping mad! You know you're going with her to the vestry meeting tonight. And you're soaking wet! (*Exits upstairs*)

DAVY
The Bonc.

MR JONES
The Bonc! (*he shakes his head in dismay. Exits upstairs to collect the overflowing bucket*)

DAVY
I'll go upstairs and change.

MRS JONES (*Angry*)(*Enters from the spench with a mop*)
Where have you been? We should have left half an hour ago! Oh, never mind, it's too wet anyway. (*Exasperated*) Well! Where have you been?

DAVY
With Michael and Eddie.

MRS JONES (*she hits Davy*)
You said you was going to the library! With Michael and Eddie, indeed! And that John, I bet! You know it's Chapel on a Wednesday night! It's too late to go out now. Take your pullover off while I get you a cup of tea, it'll warm you up a bit.

(*She takes hers and Ruth's hat and coat off*)

MR JONES (*Enters from staircase with bucket of water and pours water down the sink*)
It's coming through where the slate's missing. Mam was getting worried about you, she thought you run off to sea, gone to Liverpool and caught a boat to South America, you should be in the middle of the Irish Sea by now, according to her.

MRS JONES
Oh, be quiet will you, it's not funny. Fool!

MR JONES
All right, all right. Your mam's right you know, for once. (*Under his breath*) You should be more considerate, look at the state of you. Where have you been, anyway?

(*DAVY takes off his shoes and socks*)

DAVY
Just on the bonc, that's all. It poured down and there was nowhere to shelter so we all got soaked.

MRS JONES (*to MR JONES*)
Hurry up with that bucket or we'll be getting another soaking,

(*Exit Mr Jones upstairs with the newly empty bucket*)

What was you doing up there anyway, if the watchman catches you, you'll be for it!
And we'll have Sergeant Rees knocking on the door for everybody to see!

MR JONES (*Entering from upstairs.*) (*Nervously*)
You know you're not to go on the bonc, Davy, you've been told often enough. If old Jack
catches you he'll be calling me over and giving me a lecture. He's a right know-all just
because he won a medal in the war, you'd think he owned the place. What was you doing,
anyway? (*Sitting on a chair*)

DAVY
Looking for rabbits.

MR JONES
Looking for rabbits!

MRS JONES
Looking for rabbits!

DAVY
Yes, there's hundreds up there, Michael takes his dog and we chase them and we set up a
target and throw stones at it, nothing much.

MR JONES (*Throws a ball at DAVY, a woollen hat stuffed with newspaper*)
Game of footy?

DAVY (*Catches it and kicks it. It hits Taid or a picture or an ornament. W.H.Y.*)
Hurrah! Goal! Dixie Dean!

MRS JONES
If you break any of those ornaments, you'll be for it, you just wait and see! (*She scowls at
MR JONES*) You should have more sense!

MR JONES (*He slumps down in his chair*)
Put it away, Davy, we don't want to upset Mam. (*Pulling a face, he opens a cigarette packet
and takes out a picture card*) Here you are, another one for your collection. (*He lights a
cigarette*)

DAVY
Who is it?

MR JONES
Jack Dempsey, No.14.

DAVY
Oh, good, I haven't got him.

RUTH (SHINO)
Show me the picture of when you was a boxer, Dada.

MR JONES (*to Davy*)
When I was a boxer, those were the days. (*He spars playfully with RUTH*) I was good an all, I went three rounds with Johnny Basham, British Champion he was!

DAVY
Johnny who?

MR JONES
Johnny Basham! That was his name, Basham! Yeah! British Champion and European Champion he was! But he couldn't catch me, I was too quick for him. (To MRS JONES) He was stationed in the barracks same time as me, just after the war. Let's see your cards, Davy.

(*DAVY takes them from the drawer*)

MR JONES (*Takes the collection of cards from Davy*)
There you are, that's me.

RUTH (compares the face on the card with her father's face)
But it doesn't look like you, Dada.

MR JONES
Well, I was a lot younger then, wasn't I, Mama. (*He gives her a crafty smile*)
Here, Davy. (*He returns the cards to DAVY*)

MRS JONES (*Impatiently*)
Show her the one when you was in the Army.

MR JONES
That one! It's in tatters, that's done the rounds all right! Davy! Go and get my photo out of the parlour sideboard, it's in the top drawer…with my collars and tie.

MRS JONES (*Waiting for DAVY to exit*) (*Looking despairingly at Taid*)
Dad can't look after himself anymore, he's worse than ever, he'll have to stay and live here with us. He can't go back to his old place and I'll not let them take him to the Workhouse. When I gave him his dinner today he was staring at the wall talking to something or other.

MR JONES
Stay here? There's not enough room for us, where are we going to put him? (*Grumbling*)
There's not enough room.

MRS JONES
Then we'll have to make room! Did you hear what I said, he needs to be looked after, he can sleep with Davy in his room and Ruth can come in with us.

MR JONES
Oh no!

MRS JONES
Well where else can he go? The Workhouse? He is your father!

ARTHUR (*Knocking on the front door*)
Anyone home? (*Enter Arthur, Mr Jones's brother, carrying a rain-sodden parcel, the paper wrapping ripped and torn. A puff of smoke rises from the fire. He puts it on the table and goes back into the hallway and re-enters the kitchen, more puffs of smoke, with another bundle and places it on the table. He takes off his coat and James Cagney-style hat.*)
It's like a monsoon out there!

MRS JONES
Hello, Arthur, what's that you've got there?

ARTHUR
Well let me get my coat off first and I'll show you. It's pouring out there, I'm soaked! It's a surprise, you'll see.

(*Arthur goes over to Taid*)

MRS JONES
Looks like a bundle of rags to me!

ARTHUR
Hello, Dad, how are you?
(*No answer as DAVY rushes over to unwrap the rain-sodden parcels*)
Wait a minute, Davy, I want to talk to Dad first. Dad. Dad. (*Still no answer*) Hoi, what's all this water? Noah's Ark! (*He kicks the bucket and looks up*) Haven't you fixed that slate yet, you'll have the ceiling coming down at this rate. I know these houses are being demolished in a few months, but there's no need to bring it down while you're still living in it!
(*Despondently, ARTHUR walks over to the table. He cheers up as he shows DAVY the contents of one of the parcels*) Look at these. I got some more books for you, Schoolboy Annual 1931. I know it's a bit old but it's got some good stuff in it, how to make a camera, how to make a windmill. Eh! You'll like this, How to make a Wireless. It's the best university you can have, Davy, your own library!

(*DAVY stacks the books on the sideboard.*)

MRS JONES
Now show us what's in the other pile!

DAVY (*unwrapping the bundle, back to audience*)
It's a gramophone! (*Triumphantly*)

MRS JONES
A what?

DAVY
A gramophone, Mam! (*The horn falls off*)

MRS JONES
Yes… well I can see it's not the hooter off Doctor Ryan's car! But what's it doing here?

ARTHUR
We got it from Fred the Battery Shop, only half a crown, and some records; doesn't work, though.

MRS JONES
Oh, not more junk, you haven't fixed the crystal wireless set yet. (*She points to the wireless on the sideboard*)

ARTHUR (*He winds the handle, it comes off in his hand. Exasperation!*)
Davy will get it working, it's just the mechanism come loose. And I got some proper cable for the wireless aerial. (*He puts it on the sideboard*)

DAVY
It just needs a nut and bolt and some screws tightening.

ARTHUR
We'll get it working, don't you worry, won't we, Davy! And look at all these records, Benvenuti, he's Italian, Davy, sings opera.

DAVY (*reading the record label*)
'Where Corals Lie.' What are corals, Dad?

MR JONES
They're like seashells, I think. They're black.

ARTHUR
No, Albert, that's coal!

MRS JONES
No, that's jet what you're talking about, that's the stuff people used to have brooches made out of to commemorate old Queen Victoria. Corals are red. Nain used to have a lovely brooch made out of it, but I don't know where it is now, I think it's fallen down the back of the cupboard, I'll have to clear it out one of these days. (*She looks at the wall cupboard*) Before we go!

DAVY (*Looking at the record and mispronouncing Gigli.*)
This one says 'Giggly'.

ARTHUR (*corrects Davy's pronunciation*)
Gigli. He's Italian. Here's one by Caruso.

DAVY
What, Robinson Crusoe?

ARTHUR
No! Enrico Caruso, he's Italian as well!

MRS JONES (*sarcastically*)
Oh good, we'll be able to have a concert party then, won't we, move them off the table if you please, you'll be having your Oxo soon! You can do it later.

DAVY (*in a pleading tone*)
Aw, can't we get it working first, aw, Uncle Arthur.

ARTHUR
Better do as your Mam says.

(*She makes the Oxo*)

MR JONES
I'm getting splitting headaches at times. I'm sure it's that bloody pit, it's that black powder they use, a lot of the lads are complaining. There's really bad air in that place, it stinks like an old sewer and it's bloody dangerous, too, I'm sure they haven't taken proper air measurements for weeks and I've seen Father Christmas more times than I've seen the manager.

ARTHUR
Bonsall! He's a bloody waste of time. Too busy drinking tea with the Management.

MR JONES
He should be down there every day, I'm sure nobody's been down our end of the section for a fortnight.

MRS JONES
Well talk to the Union!

MR JONES
Ah, you know they're a waste of time. We need somebody from Lancashire. Anyway, I'm not going to stick my neck out if nobody else will. Ha. Union. Ha. What's the point, the bosses will only ignore you or brand you a troublemaker. We haven't even got a Safety Committee worth the name, you know, yesterday we fired a hundred shots and nobody cleared the face, it was like being back in the trenches, bang, bang, bang all bloody day long.

MRS JONES
That's criminal, every man should be cleared out, that's the law! Even I know that.

ARTHUR
They're not fit to look after the ponies.

MR JONES
The ponies are better looked after than we are! Well the men are not going to waste time looking for shelter when there's money to be made. Anyway, I'm not going to say anything, I'm not going to rock the boat. That's the fireman's job. You know, last week…

MRS JONES (*impatiently*)
Drink this, will you. If you're not going to do anything about it, it's no use going on about it, is it?

ARTHUR (*speaking in a low voice so as not to annoy Mrs Jones*)
It's no wonder you never see the bosses down your end. They're always up in the North District. I'm sick of seeing them there 'cos when they're there they never sort things out proper.

MR JONES
Well, what can they do, it costs money and they haven't got the money. People say they made no profit again last year.

ARTHUR
No money! No profit! What do you think pays for those big cars they drive around in, aye, and those chauffeurs to drive them? And those mansions they live in on Grosvenor Road! No money my arse!

(*He sees MRS JONES looking disapprovingly*)

MR JONES
Well, I'm telling you, there's something going to go badly wrong one of these days. (*To SHINO*) Hey, where are you going with that bottle? I'll give you a ha'penny for it.

MRS JONES
What do you want that for?

MR JONES
Work. It's as hot as hell on the face, we're all drinking like camels. Once I start I can't stop. As soon as it goes in, it comes out again! Oh, that reminds me, have you seen my old football shorts, I'll be wearing those in future. It's too hot for my corduroys.

MRS JONES
Give me that bottle. (*She takes it from Shino*) You can't take that down with you! I'll get a proper can when I go into town.

(*Davy gets tools from dresser and starts repairing the gramophone*)

ARTHUR
I've got an old one you can have.

MR JONES
Right, but I'll still give you a ha'penny for it. (*He pulls a coin from his pocket and gives it to Ruth with a playful pat on the head*)

MRS JONES
I'll look after that. (*She takes the ha'penny whilst RUTH looks sadly at her empty hand. MRS JONES puts the coin into a vase.*)

MR JONES
You're worse than the rent man, ah well, easy come, easy go.
(*He finds another ha'penny and gives it to RUTH secretly and puts his finger to his lips.*)

(EXIT RUTH)

MRS JONES
Are you staying for a paned? (*Cup of tea*)

ARTHUR
No, I've got to go, I promised to meet Jean tonight, we're going to the club.

MRS JONES
You can't go in this weather, you'll be blown away, she won't want to go neither, not in this rain. You might as well stay here and fix this gramophone thing. When you've fixed that you can have a go at the wireless, it's been stuck there for a fortnight and I haven't heard a thing!

ARTHUR
OK. Alright, Davy, get some spanners… oh, and a screwdriver.

DAVY
I've already fixed it!

ARTHUR (*Shocked at Davy's speed.*)
Oh, righto! (*He picks up a record sleeve.*) We'll have you singing along to… Handel's Messiah in no time. Oh no, that goes on for ages! (*He picks up a different record sleeve.*) No, what about 'Where Corals Lie'? I've never heard that one. Well here we go. (*The record is placed on the turntable and the music plays 'Where Corals Lie'. After a few moments the sound of scratching on the record. ARTHUR takes it off.*)

MRS JONES
Oh, shame, I liked that. Put another one on.

ARTHUR
Nah, I've got to go now, rain or no rain. I'll see you in a few days' time. And we'll fix that wireless, Davy. Goodbye, all. Goodbye, Dad. (*No answer. He shakes his head and puts his coat on. EXIT to front door with MR JONES.*)

MRS JONES
It's time you two were in bed, come on, up the wooden hills.

(*MR JONES enters, he puts his ear to the party wall. The sound of arguing is heard through the party wall.*)

MRS HOPKIN
Liar! (*A plate smashes, a chair is dragged, a baby cries, a woman screams.*) No money again, money for beer but no money for the rent man.

MR HOPKIN
Shut up, woman! (*A door bangs.*)

MR JONES (*His ear to the wall.*)
They're at it again.

MRS JONES
I don't know how she puts up with it, God bless her.

MR JONES
What can she do, leave him? And then what… end up in the Workhouse?

MRS JONES
What are we going to do with Dad?

MR JONES
What? You mean the Workhouse?

MRS JONES
No! Now, where's he going to sleep?

MR JONES
Dad, Dad. (*He shakes TAID*) Leave him there, put a blanket over him, he'll be alright.

MRS JONES
Don't be ridiculous, we can't leave him there. Put him on the couch, come on Dad, on the couch.

(*They move over to the couch and settle TAID in for the night. MR JONES inspects the record 'Where Corals Lie'.*)

MR JONES
It's got some grit on it. (*He rubs it off and plays it.*)

(*LIGHTS FADE. MUSIC FADES. THE SOUND OF DRIPPING WATER INCREASES.*)

CURTAINS

ACT 1

SCENE 2

ARTHUR (*Banging on the front door*)
Halloo! It's me!

MR JONES (*Enter Arthur*)
Ah, it's Mr Marconi. (*sarcastically*) Come to fix that wireless have you?

ARTHUR
Yes, yes. Sorry I'm late!

MR JONES
About time! It's been here for two weeks and I haven't heard a thing yet.

MRS JONES (*looking at the clock*)
It's nearly time for bed.

ARTHUR
Where's Ruth?

MRS JONES
She went to bed an hour ago.

ARTHUR
I've been busy. I got some spare valves, Davy, just in case! Test them, Davy! (*He waves the valves triumphantly*) Hello Dad. (*He stops in his tracks*) What are you doing that for, Dad? (*Taid is cutting a piece of paper from the News of the World and folds it and stuffs it under the brim of his cap.*)

TAID
It's the football results, I want to check them later with my pools coupon when I get the time.

ARTHUR
I know (*emphasise*) what you're doing, Dad! You're making those fags again aren't you, using that weed from Tommy Price's allotment.

TAID
It's good stuff, well it is for what I want it for.

ARTHUR
It's dock leaves, Dad, even tramps wouldn't smoke that stuff. You could fumigate the shed with that muck!

TAID
It's a lot cheaper than buying a packet of Woodbines.

ARTHUR
They only cost thruppence!

TAID
Yeah, but I haven't got thruppence.

ARTHUR
Well don't light up when I'm here, it stinks the house out. (*He takes his hat and coat off whilst Davy puts the wireless on the table, impatient to repair it.*)

TAID
I won't, I won't. Well, let's have one of yours, then. (*Impatiently*)

ARTHUR
I haven't got any, I don't smoke anymore!

TAID
Don't smoke. Humph!

(*ARTHUR flops down on the chair and stretches out self-confidently*)

ARTHUR
Look at this, I've got fifty pounds.

MRS JONES
Where did you get all that?

ARTHUR
Never mind, I saved it, didn't I, no drinking, no smoking, living like a monk. I'll be writing off to the steamship company to buy my ticket for America.

MRS JONES
America! So that's what you've been up to! That's what all those letters was about!

MR JONES (*mock serious*)
America of all places. It's Russia you should be going to. Russia is the country of the future.

MRS JONES
But they're killing people in Russia.

MR JONES
So what? What happened in the War? Thousands slaughtered for bugger all. Our lot blessed the guns so that they'd be better at killing German workers and at the same time was all for keeping us British workers in our place. They're creating a new society in Russia. A just society. No unemployment there, lad. No, not in Russia. Anyway, you can't make an omelette without breaking eggs.

ARTHUR
What's that supposed to mean? Anyway, what do you know about omelettes? You've never had one. Hey, you haven't been calling in at the Golf Club for tea, have you?

MR JONES
Ha, very funny. Listen, Russia will show the world one day.

ARTHUR
Look. I'm not interested in Russia. It's America I'm going to. There's no point in staying here. You work your guts out all week and at the end of it you're still only one step away from the Poor House.

TAID
Poor in pocket, yes, but rich in God's benefactions.

ARTHUR
Oh, bloody hell.

MR JONES
America, huh. There's a lot of trouble there just now between the bosses and the Unions.

ARTHUR
Well, haven't I just said there's work there for reliable men. I won't be joining no bloody union. If they want to strike, let them! I want to work!

DAVY (*after checking the wiring and valves*)
These valves are okay, Uncle Arthur.

MR JONES
If you go as scab labour, your children will be known as scabs, or whatever they call them in America, for years to come. You don't want that, do you? You might be able to bear it, but what about your kids? A lousy inheritance if you ask me. Look what happened to those lot at Plas Power after they worked through the strike. There's people still won't talk to them and that was twelve years ago.

ARTHUR
Well! I'll be glad to get away from Dad and his bloody Bible for one thing, and…well…I don't want to be living like this for the rest of my life. I want a place of my own.

MRS JONES (*angrily reacting to 'Bloody Bible'*)
Well you don't have to go to America for that. You don't even have to leave the pit. You can take some lodgings in the town.

ARTHUR
What, four to a bed. Two on the night shift and two on days. No thank you.

MRS JONES
No, I don't mean that place on the Beast Market. No, that nice Mrs Thomas near the Park.

ARTHUR
No, it's no good. My mind's made up. Jack's doing alright, I can tell you. He's even got a car. It would take me a hundred years in this place to afford one.

MR JONES
But you're on the best bonus you've ever had. They're pulling coal out of Gresford as if there's no tomorrow. I don't know where it's all going!

ARTHUR
Ah, that's the trouble. At this rate, the Dennis will be exhausted in a few years and then what am I going to do? No, I've told you, my mind's made up. I'm going!

MRS JONES
Well before you go, sort out this wireless or it will be going in the bin!

DAVY (*shocked*)
Mam!

ARTHUR (*to Davy*)
Don't worry, we'll get it going… if they'll let me. (*looking at Mr and Mrs Jones impatiently*)

MRS JONES (*perplexed*)
America. When are you thinking of going?

ARTHUR
In the New Year

MRS JONES
Do you have to be in such a hurry, can't you leave it until, well, maybe the middle of next year?

ARTHUR
No, my number's come up. It might be too late by then. I might not get another chance. The Immigration Department is very strict about such things.

MRS JONES
What about Jean?

ARTHUR
Of course, I've talked it over with her. I…I suggested we get married.

MRS JONES (*amazed*)
What!

ARTHUR
Before going…but there's no chance.

MR JONES

I'm not surprised! Knowing her mother she would have something to say about that! She's been brought up different, spoiled if you ask me, her being the only child.

MRS JONES
You must know what her parents are like. I know what her mother's like, she'd have a fit if you stood on her doorstep, you'd swear you was standing on her grave she makes so much fuss, she's always scrubbing it!

DAVY
Uncle Arthur, when are we going to start on the wireless!

ARTHUR
In a minute!

MRS JONES (*Mr Jones beckons to Mrs Jones regarding Taid*) Come on, Dad, time for bed. (*They help him to the stairs. Mrs Jones takes Taid upstairs. Mr Jones and Arthur look on despairingly.*)

ARTHUR
Goodnight, Dad! I'll have to be off soon myself, I got an early shift tomorrow. We'll have to leave it till after. (*pointing to the wireless.*)

DAVY
Oh, come on, have a go!

ARTHUR (Arthur checks Hobby Annual 1931) You've got these wires crossed. (*Arthur rearranges wires, the valves spark into action with a crackle and a lot of 'mush'*)

MR JONES
I can't hear anything. (*He puts his ear near the speaker.*)

ARTHUR
Give it a chance, it's got to warm up first!

MR JONES
Hs's probably tying his dickie-bow, they say them BBC types wear a dickie-bow to do their talking. Humph. (*He bangs it.*)

ARTHUR
Don't do that, it's a wireless, not a door knocker! (*The valves pop and all goes quiet.*) Hell! That's it, we'll have another go tomorrow! I got to go! (*Impatiently.*) (*Arthur puts on his cap and coat*) I got to be up at four. Goodnight, all, we'll look at it tomorrow. (*He rubs Davy's head playfully.*) (*Exit with Mr Jones. Front door bangs. Re-enter Mr Jones. Mrs Jones enters from upstairs.*)

MRS JONES
Well what do you think about that, America! (*She stands rigidly in shock.*)

MR JONES

He'll never make it, he gets seasick on the Marine Lake.

(*They both sit down*)

MRS JONES
Thank goodness she wouldn't go to America with him. I don't think she should marry him at all.

MR JONES
Why?

MRS JONES
Why? Oh it's not that I don't want her to go to America, it looks a marvellous place from seeing it on the pictures and it's not that I don't want her to marry Arthur, he's a good enough man, better than a lot, no, it's just that I don't want to see her marry a miner. I don't want to sound rude about Jean but she's just not strong enough, she's a bit of an old maid, isn't she? How old is she anyway? (*Mr Jones shrugs his shoulders*) It doesn't matter whether it's here or in America, it's all the same for a miner's wife. The same dirt, the same scrubbing, the same worry, the same fear. After a few years it would break the girl, I know, I've seen it before with other women harder than her, and what for? She'll never find any joy, not for long, anyway. I'll never let Ruth marry a collier, not as long as she lives in this house I won't! We're outcasts, all of us, we're not like ordinary people, well, not the better off sort, anyway. They can tell we're mining people, we carry the pit with us everywhere we go. She wouldn't want that, she's different. She's been brought up different.

MR JONES
Have you finished! Cor, here endeth the lesson! Your mother was right, you should have married a minister, not a miner.

MRS JONES (*angrily*)
Oh you! Fool!

MR JONES
Haven't you sorted out that contraption yet. It'll be me throwing it in the bin, not your mother!

MRS JONES
Yes, put that away now. Time for bed, you'll damage your eyes. (*Mrs Jones exits towards the stairs.*)

(*Davy continues to fiddle with the knobs. Various sounds are heard. Classical music, BBC types with Oxford accents.*)

MR JONES
Turn it off, I don't want to listen to them. (*Foreign languages, Hitler etc*) Get that bloody German off! (*The last few bars of God Save the King. Silence.*)

(*Mr and Mrs Jones turn to listen. Lights down. Valve lights stay on in the style of painter Joseph Wright of Derby (1734-1797) (Another argument can be heard next door.*)

ACT 1

SCENE 3

NEXT DAY. THE JONES'S BACK KITCHEN. MRS JONES, TAID AND DAVY.

(*Ruth opens the door holding Topsy, her woolly doll/animal. Neighbour enters with a black eye.*)

MRS HOPKIN
It's me again, Mrs Jones.

MRS JONES
Hello, cariad. Have things not been going well for you? That's a nasty bruise you got there. Have you seen the doctor?

MRS HOPKIN
Don't be daft, Mrs Jones. I'm not Mary Pickford, you know!

MRS JONES
Of course not. Let's dab a bit of TCP on it.

MRS HOPKIN
It's not my eye I've come about. I'm sorry to bother you again but I haven't got a crumb in the house for the kids and I've got no milk for the baby. He's driving me mad. Would you…

MRS JONES
Don't worry yourself, Mary. I've got some bread left over and the milk will be coming round soon, so you can have some of that and all. Has he gone to work this morning?

MRS HOPKIN
No fear. He's still lying on the kitchen floor where he fell over last night. The big useless heap. He's still got his boots on and I'm not taking those off while he's drunk; it's like playing with a double-barrel shotgun. He swung at me last night, broke that lovely teapot Mam gave me when I got married. It belonged to old Nain Bala. It must've been a hundred years old. Bloody drunken swine.

MRS JONES (*gives her a jug of milk*)
Here you are then, and a butty jam for the little ones.

MRS HOPKIN
Thank you, Mrs Jones. I don't know what I'll do when you leave. Maybe we'll be neighbours in the new houses.

MRS JONES (*unenthusiastically*)
Yes, maybe.

MR HOPKIN (*banging at the front door. Mr Hopkin shouts*)
Hello! Is my Mary there? (*Enters the kitchen*) Sorry to barge in like this, Mrs Jones. I thought I'd find you here, I've told you not to come moithering the neighbours, what you doing here anyway?

MRS HOPKIN
I needed some milk for the baby.

MRS JONES
Just remember you're in my house now, Jack Hopkin!

MR HOPKIN
Of course, Mrs Jones. (*An aside*) There's money enough on the mantelpiece.

MRS HOPKIN
There was none this morning.

MR HOPKIN (*still inebriated from last night*)
Don't you listen to her, Mrs Jones, she's a right little schemer, she'll tell you anything, won't you, Mary, what's the matter, lost your tongue, you had plenty to say last night.

MRS JONES
Look, I can't be having you two arguing, you'll be upsetting the children, I'm sorry but you'll have to go now, I'm sorry.

MR HOPKIN
Of course, Mrs Jones. (*To Mary*) See what you done, upsetting Mrs Jones. (*They start to exit.*) Oi! Have you got a licence for that? (*He points to the wireless.*)

MRS JONES
A what?

MR HOPKIN
A licence. You need a licence for one of those things, it's a wireless, isn't it?

MRS JONES
Yes but…a licence!

MR HOPKIN
You better get one quick, if old Sergeant Rees knows you got one he'll send one of his clodhoppers to check on you, you'd be breaking the law, you wouldn't want that would you, Mrs Jones. (*Sarcastically*)

MRS JONES (*Milk bell rings with Mr and Mrs Hopkin exiting.*)
That's Mrs Morgan with the milk, she's early! Davy, take the jug and get a pint, there's threepence on the table, and hurry! (*She points to the table as she ushers the Hopkins' out. Exit Davy.*) (*Mr Hopkin turns and Mrs Hopkin exposes her black eye to Mrs Morgan.*)

MR HOPKIN (pointing to the wireless)
It'll never catch on around here, it's only for the Toffs. (*They both exit*)

MRS MORGAN
Yoo-hoo! Can I come in, oh, I see you got visitors. (*Hesitantly*) I just spoken to your David outside, he said you was helping old Mr Jones get up so I thought I could help you by just coming in, sort of and…and sorting out the milk for you. (*Enter Davy with the jug and she*

fills it from her own and groans with the effort.) I see her from next door has got a black eye. Again! (*She waves the threepenny piece.*) It's not threepence, it's one and threepence what you owe, Mrs Jones!

MRS JONES
Is it! Goodness, whatever am I thinking of, of course! (*She hurriedly searches for the extra money*)

MRS MORGAN
That's the second pair of shoes I've worn out in six months and on the top of that, my leg's inflamed it is, but what can't be cured must be endured, isn't that right Mr Jones? (*speaking to Taid. Taid ignores her.*) All right, is he?

MRS JONES
Why don't you get Mr Milk to do the round some days, he can push the milk cart, surely. It would take some of the strain off you.

MRS MORGAN
Him! He couldn't push a pram, anyway, I couldn't trust him, he'd be on his back by dinner time, what with The Black Lion, The Castle, The Rollers (*she counts the pubs on her fingers*) It would be a free jug of milk for a pint of beer at every one of them. Yes indeed, he'd be on his back!

MRS JONES
Well, just let him walk beside you and…

MRS MORGAN
Walk! Him! Walk as far as The Black Lion, that's all he can manage. He can't even change a light bulb now, he says climbing the step ladder makes him giddy.

MRS JONES
Who looks after the dairy, you know, the cow and such things?

MRS MORGAN
Me, of course! On my way here I passed those kids in Furnace Row, they're damn pests, always wanting tick. It's their parents that put them up to it!

MRS JONES
They're so poor, Mrs Milk.

MRS MORGAN
If they can afford beer, they can afford milk, sending their kids out with their crafty little smiles and shoes three times too big for their feet, proper little Charlie Chaplins, well they're not fooling me. They'll get no tick off me. No money, no milk!

MRS JONES
I don't know how those little ones manage.

MRS MORGAN
They manage all right! They manage to make a racket all day long, banging doors, banging cans, banging the railings with their sticks, running around all day they are, banging and shouting even on a Sunday! Heathens! They manage all right! They should be in the Workhouse by rights but they're afraid of having to wash! You're always reading the paper!

TAID (*pretending to ignore her*)
Mmm.

MRS MORGAN
I said, you're always reading the paper Mr Jones. I bet you read the advertisements as well. Hoi, what's all these pencil marks on the racing page, you're not doing the horses, are you? Fancy yourself as that black man with the turban, what's his name, Prince Monolulu. 'I gotta horse.' Haha. And I'll tell you something else, that Mrs Hughes talking with the insurance man again, she bleaches her hair you know, well it's obvious she's trying to look like one of them American film stars, it burns your hair you know, she'll be bald by the time she's forty. (*Taid lights a fag, smoke billows.*) What's that made of, old rubber? (*She coughs violently*)

(*Mrs Morgan picks up her milk money and makes a quick exit.*)

TAID (*waves his newspaper*)
We don't need The News of the World with her around, she knows everything!

(*Mr Jones peers around the corner of the stairs, half-undressed, just out of bed*)

MR JONES
Good, has she gone? You woke me up with all that shouting, it's like Piccadilly Circus round here!

(*Taid cuts pieces of paper out of The News of the World. Mr Jones walks over to Taid. Taid cuts up pieces of leaf and stuffs it into a tin/pipe/cigarette*)

MR JONES
What's that stuff you using, Dad?

TAID (*he shows the contents of his tobacco tin*)
Tom Price grows it on his allotment.

MR JONES
How many times have I told you, that's not tobacco., it's dock leaf, you're as daft as he is. I can't understand why you smoke that stuff.

TAID
Well you're wrong there see cos it is tobacco, well sort of. Dai brought the seeds back from South America when he was in the Merchant Navy.

MR JONES
South America! That stuff is even worse than dock leaves. The Indians dip their arrows in the stuff, it's poisonous! I don't mind if you want to poison Mrs Morgan but not us.

TAID
Don't worry, I'm not going to smoke it.

MR JONES (*shakes his head in dismay*) (*He returns to bed and turns at the foot of the stairs*)
Keep your noise down, I've got to go to work this afternoon. (*Exit, upstairs*)

MRS JONES (*to Ruth*)
Well I'm going to the shop, Shino, you stay here with Davy till I come back. Dad, come and sit in the parlour in your armchair, it's warmer there and the sun's shining so you can read your paper easier. (*Exit Taid and Mrs Jones. Davy and Ruth remain.*)

JOHN (*John Hopkin knocks on the window. Davy beckons him in.*)
Hey Davy, how you doing, I just saw your mam go out, how long is she going to be, I don't want her catching me here, she dunna like me.

DAVY
I've got to look after Ruth until she comes back.

JOHN
How long's that going to be?

DAVY
I don't know, not long, depends if she sees someone from Chapel, then she'll be all day!

JOHN
Bloody hell, Davy, what you doing with all these books, you don't read them, do you?

DAVY
I don't really want them but my uncle keeps bringing them cos I tell Mam I'm going to the library all the time so she thinks I'm book daft, but I only do it so that I can get out of the house, she wouldn't let me out if she knew I was with you. Eh but look what I found in this book. (*He opens a book*) How to make a wireless, how to make a telescope, a catamaran.

JOHN
What's a catamaran?

DAVY
Oh, like a sailing boat. But I want to make a wireless, Uncle Arthur will show me.

JOHN (*He stretches out in the armchair*)
Bloody hell, I wish I was back in school, sitting on my arse all day… (*He jumps up excitedly.*) Hey, look at this!

DAVY
What?

JOHN
The inside of me coat! I've cut the lining so I can carry a load of apples with nobody seeing. It's an old poacher's trick. Naccy innit. Come on down to the Vicarage and pinch a few. I want some apples for the ponies down the pit, especially Soldier, he's my favourite.

DAVY

Oh, I don't fancy that! When I went past there the other day, there was a blinking big dog chained up by that black shed at the side of the house as you go up the hill. It was a nasty looking thing.

JOHN

Don't worry about him. He's chained up, isn't he.

DAVY

Yeah, but it's not only that. What about the hedge. It's all thorns. Now that they've blocked up the hole on the corner you got to climb over the hedge and if I rip my trousers again my Dad'll belt me.

JOHN

Oh come on! You're not scared are you, Davy? (*Emphasise*)

DAVY

Alright. If you will, I will, but you got to promise if we get seen you won't run off and leave me by myself.

JOHN

Course I won't! (*John sees some cigarette ends in an ashtray*) Hey, let's make a fag!

DAVY

Oh no! Me mam will be back soon and she'll know you been smoking, she'll go mad!

JOHN

She'll never know, I'll blow the smoke up the chimney. Here, watch this. (*He unravels the cigarette ends and wraps the tobacco in a cigarette paper and lights it*)

RUTH

If Mama knows you smoking, you'll be in trouble.

JOHN

She won't know unless you tell her, Shino. (*Emphasise*) (*He blows the smoke up the chimney*)

RUTH

You mustn't do that, Father Christmas will be coming down soon.

JOHN

Bugger Father Christmas, I'll burn his little arse for him. (*He twists his cigarette menacingly.*)

(*Bang, the front door. Bang, the parlour door. Mrs Jones talks to Taid.*)

Blydi hell, it's Mrs Jones! I'm going. I'll see you at Top Road, Davy. (*Exit back door in a hurry*)

(Enter Mrs Jones, she stops at the door, she senses that something is going on.)

DAVY
I'm going out, Mam!

MRS JONES
Wait a minute! I've only just got in!

DAVY
I got to go, Mam, I'm going to the library before they close for dinner.

MRS JONES
You'd better not be with that John Hopkin, he's always up to mischief.

DAVY
He won't be in the library, Mam, he can't read! *(Exit quickly.)*

LATER THAT DAY. LYING ON A GRASSY BANK AFTER THEIR RAID ON THE
VICARAGE ORCHARD.

JOHN
Can I help you, young man? *(Mimicking the vicar's accent)* I jumped over that fence like one
of them horses in the Grand National! Ripped the arse out of my trousers though! *(He reveals
the rip)*

DAVY
Coo, I nearly peed myself, where the hell did he come from? Do you think he recognised us?

JOHN
Nah, not me, anyway. I've never been to church, bah, he can't do anything, he doesn't scare
me. You did well, straight past the dog and out of the gate! Lucky he was on a chain or you'd
have had the arse ripped out of your trousers as well!

DAVY
But he might have recognised me! If he tells me Mam she'll go mad!

JOHN
He doesn't know you, the old bugger's nearly blind, he's got them glasses as big as goldfish
bowls. Everybody looks daft like in the Hall of Mirrors in the fairground. You know, like
that. *(He moves his hands to form strange shapes.) (Davy looks bemused.)* Don't worry about
it, Davy, when the revolution comes we'll be putting his sort up against a wall and shooting
them.

DAVY
You shouldn't talk like that about the Reverend, John. He's a man of God. Don't you ever go
to church…or chapel?

JOHN

Nah! You wouldn't catch me in one of them places, I can't bear the stink, for one thing, all Brasso and floor polish! Anyway, me Dad says religion is the opium of the people. He's read all the books on it, Karl Marx and that.

DAVY

What's opium, John?

JOHN (*He doesn't know*)

Um…um… How many did you get? (*John opens his pockets*)

DAVY (*He empties his pockets*)

I've only got a few.

JOHN

Ugh, you dropped most of yours, I'm okay, I've still got plenty. Soldier will have a good feed this week, I'll give the rest to me Mam and she can make a pie with them.

DAVY

You can't eat them, they're overripe and rotten. (*Winter windfalls*)

JOHN

The ponies can!

DAVY

What will you say if she asks you where you got them from?

JOHN

Nothing, I won't say nothing, she's not interested, she likes apple pie as much as I do.

DAVY

Do you think God will punish us?

JOHN

Punish us? God? Don't talk daft, Davy. It's Sergeant Rees you want to worry about. Miserable old bugger! He'd jail his own grandmother for riding a bike without lights.

DAVY

But his grandmother can't ride a bike, she's over ninety!

JOHN (*Exasperated at Davy's naivety*)

Oh, never mind.

(*The winter sun begins to set as they lie down on the bank and watch the spoil buckets moving above their heads and casting shadows. Clickety-click, clickety-click as a bucket passes over a pylon.*)

JOHN

You know, when I was a kid I used to dream about riding in them buckets, high up in the sky, away from everyone, secret like, hiding from my Dad. Now I hate the bloody sight of them!

(*The winter sun sinks lower*) Bloody hell, Davy, I'm getting cold, let's go home.

EXIT

LATER THAT EVENING. THE JONES'S BACK KITCHEN. ENTER DAVY.

MRS JONES
Where have you been, and don't bother telling me a tale, you've been with that John Hopkin, haven't you! Mrs Hughes the Vicarage said she saw you taking apples at her orchard with John Hopkin. Is that right?

DAVY
Um, um…

MRS JONES
Well, did she?

DAVY
Um, um…

MRS JONES
Answer me!

DAVY
Um, um…

MRS JONES
I'll take that to mean yes! How many times have I told you to keep away from there and keep away from that John Hopkin? He's too old, you'd think that he'd have more sense now that he's working, he likes to show off in front of you boys because he's got a job at the colliery. I've told you and told you. And that Mrs Hughes, she loves to look down her nose at us, accusing us of being thieves. And she's right. Those apples aren't yours, so don't take them!

TAID
Your Mam's right, you know. The law is there to be obeyed and those that break it must answer for it. It says so in the Bible.

MRS JONES (*She takes something out of the drawer*)
Hold your hand out. Hold your hand out! (*She smacks him across the hand.*) Sit over there and don't move. (*Silence*)

MR JONES (*In an attempt to break the deathly silence*)
Those privies are overflowing again, every time there's a bit of rain.

MRS JONES
I'll be glad when we move into our new house. It's like the Black Hole of Calcutta around here at times, it's a wonder we don't get consumption. (*Washing at the sink*)

RUTH (*Lying on the floor next to Davy*)

What's consumption?

DAVY
It's when you spit out blood.

RUTH
My nose was bleeding yesterday.

DAVY
Oh, be quiet will you. I'm trying to read.

RUTH
What you reading?

DAVY (*He reads the headline*)
Her... Herr Hitler. New German Chancellor.

RUTH
What's Hitler?

DAVY (*Impatiently*)
Oh, I don't know! But Dada doesn't like the Germans, he said they killed Uncle Robert in the War and they tried to kill him as well but he was too clever for 'em and they couldn't catch him. He says they'll start another if they get the chance.

RUTH
Another what?

DAVY
Another war, dopey!

(*Ruth runs away to her mother, sulking.*)

MRS JONES
If you pair don't stop squabbling, I'll get that nasty Mr Hitler to chase you. Now stop it, I won't tell you again! (*Davy moves over to Mr Jones*) And I'll send you to Dr Barnardo's!

DAVY
Dad, do you think Hitler's aeroplanes will drop bombs on us?

MR JONES
Why are you asking a daft question like that!

DAVY
I heard Mr Griffiths and Wil taking about it down by the railway.

MR JONES
You don't want to pay any attention to them two, Mr Griffiths hasn't been right since his accident, and Wil, he was born daft, anyway, they can't reach this far, we're miles from Germany.

DAVY
But Amy Johnson got to Australia and that's further!

MR JONES
He wouldn't dare, Davy, anyway there's nothing here worth bombing.

DAVY
What about the steelworks?

MR JONES (*Impatiently*)
Look, if he does start anything, he'll be too busy bombing London to bother with us!

MRS JONES
Will you stop talking nonsense about the war, didn't you learn anything from the last one?

MR JONES
I'm just saying if he starts he'll get a thumping, that's all.

MRS JONES
A thumping, my foot! It'll be like the last one! Remember Jack Walters, he said he'd come back with a medal or a wooden leg, well he didn't come back at all, did he!

MR JONES (*Dismissively*)
Anyway, they say Hitler was a painter in the War so he won't be much use if there's another, will he! (*Mrs Jones bangs down the plates in the sink angrily.*) (*Everyone goes quiet.*) (*To Ruth*) I thought you wanted to make some Christmas decorations? (*She brings out a cardboard box from the cupboard, filled with papers, and plonks it on the table.*) Here's one of Dada's old football socks, we can make a stocking out of it and hang it from the mantelpiece.

RUTH
Will Mr Williams at the Co-op have a stocking?

MRS JONES
What are you asking that for?

RUTH
Cos David said he's got a wooden leg... why's he got a wooden leg, Mama?

MRS JONES
He lost it in the war.

RUTH
How can you lose a leg, Mama?

MRS JONES (*Irritated*)
Oh, I don't know.

RUTH
How do you write Happy Christmas?

MRS JONES
Here, I'll show you. (*She writes on a piece of paper.*) There you are, copy that.

RUTH
Mama, you never tell fibs, do you? (*She starts writing Happy Christmas on the decorations without looking up*)

MRS JONES
No...no.

RUTH
You always tell the truth, don't you?

MRS JONES
Yes, why are you asking?

RUTH
Well...Betty says Father Christmas...Father Christmas doesn't have fairies at all to help him and he has to do all the work by himself.

MRS JONES
Well never you mind what Betty says.

RUTH (*She holds her piece of card up*)
I've finished. Can I go and put it in the bedroom window now?

DAVY
You're in the back room, nobody will see it there except next door's cat!

MRS JONES
Leave her Davy, if she wants to, anyway it's time for bed. Come on up the wooden hills.

RUTH
I don't want to go to bed yet!

MRS JONES
Come on, Father Christmas won't be leaving you anything in your stocking if you're not a good girl, so get up to bed.

RUTH
But he only left me an orange and a hanky last time.

MRS JONES
Well he might leave you more things if you go to bed now. (*Exasperated*) Go to bed like a good girl, you know how long it takes you to get up in the morning. I don't want you being late for school on the last day before the holidays!

RUTH
I don't want to go to school!

MRS JONES
Don't be silly! You've got to go to school or you won't learn anything. Father Christmas won't be coming down that chimney with presents for you my girl if you carry on like this!

RUTH
There isn't a Father Christmas, Eric Hughes said so. He said they're just men dressed up. We saw two of them in the shops.

MRS JONES
Well... they're just pretend Father Christmases but the real one will be coming down that chimney on Christmas Eve, like he always does, if you behave yourself.

RUTH (*She runs over to the fireplace*)
I hope you burn your little arse, Father Christmas!

MRS JONES
What did you say, you little madam! Where did you learn language like that! Get up those stairs now!

(*Exit Ruth, running*)

CURTAINS

ACT II

SCENE 1

MRS JONES
There's a letter. (*She points to the mantelpiece.*) It's been there since yesterday.

MR JONES
I know, I put it there.

MRS JONES
Well read it and see what it says.

MR JONES
Hmmm…if it's from who I think it is. The Examination Board. (*He opens the letter.*)
They're still offering him a place at the County School, they say it's his last chance, he'll be too old by next month.

MRS JONES
I told you this would happen!

MR JONES
You know what the answer is. (*He throws the letter on the fire.*)

MRS JONES (*Retrieving it*)
His last chance! (*She reads it.*)

MR JONES
You know we can't afford it. There's books to be bought, uniform, lots of things. Anyway, we need his wages to keep the house running and feed him. Look, I want him to go to the Grammar School as much as you do, but it's not on!

MRS JONES
You're taking away the only decent chance he'll have in life.

MR JONES
Look, we can't afford it, how many times do you need telling. He'll have to be dressed up like Little Lord Fauntleroy to go to a school like that. Look where your education got you. All the sacrifices your parents made, and it nearly broke your mother's heart when you married me. A collier!

MRS JONES
Yes, but I was a girl, it's different for a boy, he can make something of himself with a Grammar School Education. You know how clever he is, mending these electrical things.

MR JONES (*Under his breath*)
We can't afford it.

DAVY (*Angrily*)
I want to work in the pit!

MRS JONES
Oh, you don't want to go to the pit really, do you. It's not too late to change your mind, you know.

DAVY
I want to go to the colliery, Mam! I want to work with Dad and Uncle Arthur!

MRS JONES
And him next door, I suppose!

DAVY
I don't want the other boys laughing at me. They're all working now. I want to be like them.

MRS JONES
You want to be like them, indeed! You want to be like him next door, more like it. Talk sense. Covered in dirt every day, I don't want to see any more black faces coming through that door. It's like watching a parade of Black and White Minstrels. I want you to get a nice job so you can come home clean. Go down the pit, indeed, you talk as if you're going down into some Aladdin's Cave. You've been listening to that John Hopkin boasting, I suppose. He makes himself out to be something special with you schoolboys.

MR JONES
He'll just have to carry on working at the shop for the time being.

MRS JONES
Let's look in The Leader, there's always shopkeepers asking for errand boys.

MR JONES
Errand boy! He's an errand boy now! He'll get nowhere running around with an apron on, he can earn ten shillings more at Gresford and increases, as long as he bucks his ideas up. With his brains he could be something in the colliery. An overman, even a manager!

MRS JONES
All the more reason for him to stay on at school and get some qualifications.

MR JONES (*Exasperated*)
We can't afford it!

MRS JONES
We could sell the piano. I never play it now.

MR JONES (*Dismayed*)
Sell the piano! It's only worth fifteen bob. We can't afford it.

MRS JONES
Well I'm not the one who goes drinking in the Roller's Arms every Saturday night!
(*Long silence*)
There's no need to rush him into pit work yet. Don't let him go underground, Albert, at least get him a job on top.

MR JONES
Anyway, he's not old enough to work underground!

MRS JONES
Well there you are then, get him a job on top!

MR JONES (*Impatiently*)
All right, all right, I'll see what I can do, I'll have to speak to the Manager, it's up to him, not me. Don't worry, Cariad, he'll probably change his mind after a few days down the pit. It will teach him a lesson, make him start thinking a bit more about his future, maybe become an electrician, now there's good money! But he's got to learn a few lessons first. Anyway, it will be a few weeks yet, they're not taking on anyone at the moment. Sell the piano, humph! I'm going for a walk. (*Angry. He moves to the door.*)

MRS JONES
You can't! You've got to be in this afternoon to say hello to the Reverend. He's coming to speak to Dad, so we'll have to put Dad in the parlour. I can't let the Reverend see this place and make sure you don't let him see that paper (*pointing to the News of the World*) I don't want him thinking we're heathens, and remember your manners, Davy, if I ask you if you would like a piece of cake, say 'No thank you'.
(*Davy reads a book at the table.*)
(*Mr Jones sits down again and starts to read the paper.*)

MR JONES
Talk to Dad, he won't get much sense there, he's been delirious for two days. Anyway, what's he coming to talk to Dad about?
(*Mrs Jones snatches the News of the World and hides it*)

MRS JONES
Oh, I don't know, it was your Dad's idea, you know what he's like, anyway never mind that, it would be nice if you were here just to show your face, after all, he is coming to see your father.

MR JONES
Even so, you're one of his flock, you can speak to him better than I can. I don't want to be stuck in the house on my afternoon off. It's all right for him, he just has to hand round the collection plate on a Sunday. I got to work for my living.

MRS JONES
You talk some rubbish at times!

MR JONES
Anyway…I've promised Davy we'll go for a walk down the fields this afternoon.
(*She hands him a cup of tea.*)
There's no milk!

MRS JONES
It's sour, you'll have to wait until Mrs Morgan gets here. (*As an afterthought*) Oh! No and I haven't got any milk for the Reverend's tea. (*A milk cart bell is heard*) Speak of the devil! Oh, thank goodness!

MR JONES
She's late, isn't she, bolt that door before the old busybody pushes herself in.

MRS JONES
No! I've got to have milk for the Reverend's tea.

MRS MORGAN (*Mrs Morgan enters, breathless*)
Sorry I'm late. Oh, I do hate letting my customers down but one of the cows got out, I had to round her up by myself. I work my fingers to the bone, but nobody appreciates it. Not working today, Mr Jones? It looks like rain. (*She points to the window*)
(*Mrs Morgan puts her jug on the table and fills Mrs Jones's jug.*)
(*Mrs Jones pretends to wash dishes in the sink*)
I see Mrs Sullivan is having another one, I wonder if it's right bringing children into this world, after my third I told him no more. If my Harry wanted another one, I'd tell him to clear off somewhere and he could have dozens of them.

MRS JONES
I'm sorry Mrs Morgan but I've got a lot on today, I'm expecting the Reverend Gower-Jenkins soon, he's coming to speak to old Mr Jones.

MRS MORGAN
Wants to make his peace with the Lord, does he! Here, let me help you finish them off. Of course, I got them new stainless-steel cutlery, made in Sheffield stamped on them, doesn't rust overnight like this old steel stuff, Dew, clever they are from Sheffield. Of course I always wash mine in carbolic, much more hygienical you know. Do you?

MRS JONES
Do you what, Mrs Morgan?

MRS MORGAN
Wash your pots and stuff in carbolic?

MRS JONES.
Carbolic! No indeed, this isn't the Workhouse, Mrs Morgan!

MRS MORGAN
Oh! ... Hoi, have you been feathering your nest?

MRS JONES
Whatever do you mean, Mrs Morgan?

MRS MORGAN
This one's got GWR stamped on it!

MRS JONES
That's very offensive, Mrs Morgan.

(*Mr Jones hides behind his paper*)

MRS MORGAN
And so's taking things you shouldn't. Only joking, I was. (*Sarcastically*) (*Without a smile*)
Hello, this one's got 'Refreshment Rooms, Chester Station' on it. (*Faux shock*)

MRS JONES
It has not. (*She snatches the knife away*)

MRS MORGAN
Joking I was, Dearie.

(*Taid starts to roll a fag*)

MRS JONES
Mrs Morgan, I'm expecting the Reverend, so...
(*Taid starts to roll out his 'tobacco'*) (*Which Mrs Morgan sees. Mrs Jones ushers Mrs Morgan to the back door. EXIT. Mrs Morgan sees the smoke billowing from Taid's fag/pipe which she wants to avoid at all costs.*)

MR JONES
Listen to her! I work my fingers to the bone, she's got fingers like pork sausages. I'd like to have seen her chasing a cow down Black Lane. What a sight! Like Fatty Arbuckle!

MRS JONES
Dad, Dad, are you awake, the Reverend will be here soon. Dad!

TAID
Yes, yes, I'm awake, I just didn't want her knowing my business.

MRS JONES
Stay in here, Dad, while I tidy the parlour before the Reverend arrives. You can speak to him in there.

TAID
Who? What? What does he want?

MRS JONES
You wanted to speak to him about your...will.

MR JONES (*Mr Jones retrieves the News of the World from its hiding place.*)
Where's the middle pages gone? Oh Dad, have you been to the lav again! Why didn't you use last week's Daily Express, everybody's read that!

MRS JONES
Oh no you don't, The Reverend will be here soon. (*She snatches the News of the World from Mr Jones and hides it.*) (*The door knocks.*) Oh no, that'll be him!

MR JONES
Come on, Davy, we'd better make ourselves scarce.
(*Exit Mr Jones through back door. Davy is slow and remains in the room.*)

MRS JONES (She tidies up)
Let him in, Davy, if it's anybody else, tell them I'm out.

(*Enter Davy and the Reverend.*)

Come in, Reverend, I'm sorry to bring you into the kitchen but I wasn't expecting you so soon.

REVEREND GOWER JENKINS
I hope it's not too inconvenient but as I was passing I thought I should call.
Good day, Mr Jones, how are you today?

(*Mrs Jones exits to the parlour to collect the best china tea service.*)

TAID
Oh, not bad, Reverend, can't complain.

REVEREND GOWER JENKINS
Good, good. (*He sits down beside Taid.*) Do you still follow the football results, I know you were a loyal supporter of the Town in your younger days. How did they get on last week?

TAID
I don't know, Reverend. I can't read the papers nowadays, my eyes, you know. Where's the paper?

REVEREND GOWER JENKINS (He retrieves the paper from its hiding place.) (He reads the football results.) Oh, they won! They seem to be doing quite well recently.

(*Enter Mrs Jones with the tray of china. She sees the Reverend reading the News of the World and falls against the door in shock.*) (*He puts the newspaper down. Mrs Jones picks it up hastily and exits with it.*)

Well now, shall we get started.

TAID
Started, started on what?

REVEREND GOWER JENKINS
You wanted me to witness your will, isn't that right? Isn't that right, Mrs Jones?
(*Mrs Jones in parlour*) Oh we seem to be alone, Mr Jones.

TAID
Good, I don't want her to know my business!

REVEREND GOWER JENKINS
Oh I'm sure she has your best interests at heart, Mr Jones. Shall we start?

TAID
Start what?

REVEREND GOWER JENKINS
Your will, Mr Jones, your will!

(*Enter Mrs Jones*)

MRS JONES
Would you like a cup of tea, Reverend?

REVEREND GOWER JENKINS
Not for me, thank you, I've just come from Mr Hopkin next door.

TAID
Oh yes, my will. Well first I want to leave two hundred to my brother Isaac, fifty to my dear old friend Enoch Davies, one hundred to my dear friend Mrs Evans the Shop, another hundred to Mr Williams…

(The Reverend interrupts)

REVEREND GOWER JENKINS
My word Mr Jones, I didn't realise you were such a prosperous man! I didn't know you had so much money! I hope you don't keep it under the mattress. (*Laughs*)

TAID
Keep what under the mattress?

REVEREND GOWER JENKINS
Your money, of course.

TAID
Money, what money, I haven't got no money. I'm not talking about money.

REVEREND GOWER JENKINS
Well what are you talking about, then?

TAID
Spraggs!

REVEREND GOWER JENKINS
Spraggs!

TAID
Yes, spraggs, nails, for nailing clogs…and shoes.

MRS JONES
Oh Dad, oh dear me! (*Long silence*)

REVEREND GOWER JENKINS
I don't think Mr Jones is in need of my services, Mrs Jones. Mr Jones, I'm afraid you must engage the services of someone… more qualified. Good day, Mr Jones, take care now. Good day Mrs Jones. (*Exit*)

MRS JONES
Oh, Dad!

TAID
Where's the Minister going?

MRS JONES
Timbuktu! To see how far it is!

TAID
Wait a minute, I haven't finished yet, I still got another five hundred to give away!

MRS JONES (*Impatiently*)
Do you want to go back to bed or are you staying here?

TAID
I'll go up, I'm feeling a bit dizzy.
(*They both move to the stairs.*)

MRS JONES (*Enter Ruth, followed by Mr Jones*)
I thought you was supposed to be going for a walk.

MR JONES
I saw Ruth, she's fallen over and cut her leg.

MRS JONES
Can you get up the stairs by yourself, Dad?

TAID
Yes, I'll be alright.

MRS JONES
Come here, Shino, let's look at that leg. (*She applies a handkerchief*)

MR JONES
The Minister just shot past me on the street, didn't say a word.

MRS JONES
It was your Dad's fault, talking about spraggs again! Talking as if they was pound notes. I think the Minister was hoping for a donation.

MR JONES
Oh that's why he looks like someone who'd found a tanner and lost a sovereign! No new electric lights for the vicarage, then! (*He lifts the lid of the china teapot.*) No tea!

MRS JONES
The Minister didn't want any, he had a cup next door.

MR JONES
Next door! What's he going there for! Has the drunken old bugger taken the pledge, then? Blydi hell! Ha! Border Breweries will be going out of business!

MRS JONES
You needn't talk about him, you spend enough time in the Rollers Arms yourself!

MR JONES
Ugh! I only have a pint and a game of dominoes. Do you think I've got a fancy woman, you talk as if I'm the Prince of Wales. I tell you what, there was only a couple of old girls in the snug last night. One was smoking a pipe and I'm sure she was stuffing it with the same muck that Taid stuffs in his pipe, the other was Florrie and she hasn't had a wash for a month. Women! (*He shakes his head in disbelief*) I'm off out. (*Exit Mr Jones, slamming the door behind him*)

MRS JONES (*Mrs Jones hurries after him.*)
(*To Davy*) I'll be back in a few minutes, look after Ruth while I'm out.
(*Exit Mrs Jones running after Mrs Jones*)

(*John Hopkin knocks on the window. Davy beckons him inside the house.*)

JOHN
Hiyah Davy, I just saw Mrs Jones going out, running after your dad, so I'm safe for the time being. (*He laughs nervously*) How you doing? Come up on the bonc to catch a few rabbits, I put a few snares up there last night. I want to see if I caught any.

DAVY
Righto, but I got to look after Ruth until me Mam comes back. She's in a bad mood.

JOHN (*Impatiently*)
Oh, how long's that going to be?

DAVY
Not long.

JOHN
You'll have to hurry up, you know she dunna like me, I don't want to be here when she comes in! (*He slumps down on a chair by the dinner table*) (*He sees the milk and bread on the table.*) Hey! Let's take some milk and sugar and some butties and we can have a bit of a feed when we get up there.

DAVY
Oh I don't know, me Mam will see that we've taken some, she's bound to notice.

JOHN
Ah, ya big baby, go on, she'll never know. Here, just watch this! (*Davy gets two bottles from the cupboard*) Get us a couple of bottles. Fill that one with water and I'll fill this with milk. (*He adds some sugar to the milk.*) (*Into the milk jug he adds the water*) There you are, the perfect crime. Ha ha! (*John lights a cigarette and hands it to Davy*)

RUTH
If Mam finds out what you been doing, you'll be in trouble.

DAVY
Well she's not going to find out, is she, not unless you tell her! If you don't like it, go away, go and play with your doll. (*Davy inhales and coughs violently. The cigarette is ejected from his mouth.*) Crikey, these cigarettes is slippy. (*He picks up the cigarette and tries again.*)

RUTH
Taid said smoking stunts your growth.

JOHN (*Mockingly*)
He should know, he's only five foot and smokes like a chimney! Ha ha!

(*A door bangs*)

DAVY
Hell, it's Mam. (*They throw their cigarettes into the fireplace*)

(*Mrs Jones enters and stares at John*)

JOHN
If you tell anyone what we done I'll cut your curls off, SHINO (*Emphasise*)
I'm just going, Mrs Jones. (*He exits quickly, confused by which door to leave by*)

(*Mrs Jones glares at the retreating John*)

MRS JONES
I've told you to keep him out of the house (*She greets Ruth*) Put the kettle on, will you, I'm gasping for a cup of tea. (*She takes her shoes off*) (*She pours the milk into the cup*) I'm sure Mrs Morgan is watering this milk!

DAVY
I'm going out now, Mam.

MRS JONES
Where are you going?

DAVY (*Exits back door*)
The library!

MRS JONES (*Mrs Jones hurries to back door*)
Keep away from that John Hopkin!

DAVY
I keep telling you, Mam, he won't be in the library, he can't read!

CURTAINS

ACT II

SCENE 11

LATER THAT DAY IN THE SIGHT AND SOUND OF THE SPOIL BUCKETS

JOHN
Shush! There they are. I think I've caught one, come on. (*They hurry across and pull a dead rabbit out of the snare*) Eh Davy, it's not a rabbit, it's a hare. (*He takes a swig from the bottle*)

DAVY
Well what's the difference?

JOHN
It's bad luck to kill a hare.

DAVY
Bad luck? Why?

JOHN
I dunno, it just is, that's all.

DAVY
Who said?

JOHN
The Gypsies when they showed me how to make a snare and catch rabbits.

DAVY
What you going to do with it?

JOHN
I dunno, you can't eat these. Bury it, I suppose. (*He scrapes the ground with his boot, puts the hare in the scrape and covers it with dirt and stones.*) I know what, let's find a hedgehog.

DAVY
A hedgehog? How you going to find a hedgehog? What do you want to find a hedgehog for?

JOHN
To eat of course, but we got to cook it first. (*He pulls out the bottle of milk triumphantly.*)

DAVY
Ugh! It's covered in spikes!

JOHN
That doesn't matter, I how to do it. you cover it in mud and then you bake it in the fire like a spud. And when you pull the mud off it, it pulls the spikes off as well.

DAVY
Ugh, I'm not hungry.

JOHN (*Disappointed*)
You never try anything! Are you going to the snob's school you was talking about? (*He takes a swig and slings the empty bottle into the undergrowth*)

DAVY
I don't think so. I'm getting a job in town until Dad gets me a job on top at the pit. That'll be in a couple of weeks' time.

JOHN (*Back to back*)
I heard a collier had his leg chopped off at Powerhall Pit, a slab fell off the roof and went straight through him. (*He waves his arm in a sweeping motion*) He'll get a few hundred quid compensation… if he's insured. Probably buy a house with it, blydi hell, big deal, and he went through the war without a scratch. (*He turns abruptly to Davy*) You must be mad wanting to come here to work when you had a chance of going to the big school in town. You could get a job with a collar and tie…and a bowler hat!

DAVY
Yeah, maybe, but… I was scared of going there, me Mam would have expected me to be top of the class but I'm not that clever. She'd have been really upset.

JOHN
Nah, she wouldn't have, not as long as you did your best.

DAVY
It's too late now. Anyway, I've got a job in town just for a couple of weeks, like I said.

JOHN
What job?

DAVY
In the Maypole Stores in High Street.

JOHN (*Amazed and disgusted*)
An errand boy, delivering Lipton's tea to old ladies! That's no job for a collier lad!

DAVY
I'm not a collier yet.

JOHN
No, but you soon will be. Come on, let's go. (*John jumps up, prances around singing 'Tosher Bailey', 1ˢᵗ verse.*)

> *Down the pit we want to go*
> *Away from school and all its woe*
> *Working hard as a collier's butty*
> *Makes us all so very happy!*
> *Did you ever see, did you ever see, did you ever see such a funny thing before.*

(*They both exit across the stage, arm in arm*)

DAVY
Oh blydi hell, it's Jack Watchman, let's get going quick.

(*Exit in a hurry in opposite directions.*)

CURTAINS

(Enter Davy, limping, with Ruth)

TAID
Why are you looking so digalon, why are you walking like that, you look like that fellow in the Co-op what lost a leg in the war. You haven't been in the wars, have you?

DAVY
No, no.

TAID
What you been doing, then?

DAVY
Well, um…

TAID
Come here.

DAVY
I got a boil on my bum. It's the seat on that Maypole Stores bike, it's broken, I can't sit on it proper and now I got this boil, but I can't tell Mam, can I?

TAID
Come on, let's see. Iesu, I'll say. It's as big as an ostrich egg. Well we'll have to get rid of that and I've got just the thing. *(Taid rummages in the drawer)* Boil some water and we'll have it sorted out before Mam gets back. Get a jam jar and you go out to play in the yard, this is no place for a girl. Go on! Off with you! *(Exit Ruth)* *(He steams the rim of the jar)* Get the steam on the end, get it really hot, turn it, that's it, go on.

DAVY
Ow, I've burnt my hand!

TAID
Here, have this cloth. That's it, now bend over this couch. Come on, drop your trousers.

DAVY
No, Taid!

TAID
Oh, come on. *(Ruth peeps around the door)* Get into the yard, you! Lift them up, then. *(Davy reluctantly lifts the leg of his trousers)* Hold tight, brace yourself, here goes!

DAVY
Aaaarrrghhhh!

TAID
Don't be a big baby. Here's some lint, wipe it. How are you feeling, lad?

DAVY
Blinking awful.

TAID
Ah well, that's to be expected. Rub some of this Tiger Balm on it and it'll soon get better.

RUTH (*Ruth enters*)
Can I have some medicine, too?

TAID (*Taid rummages in a drawer and extracts a bottle*)
Here's your medicine, little one (*pretends to take a swig from the bottle*) That's tasty, better than a bottle of Vimto, it is. If that doesn't make you better, nothing will.

RUTH (*She looks at the bottle which is still full*) But Taid, it's still in there! (*Taid pours some onto a spoon. She drinks it.*)

TAID
There, now off you go. (*Exit Ruth. Taid returns to his chair to sleep. Exit Davy, rubbing his leg. The kettle whistles. Lights down.*)

(*Later. Enter Ruth.*)

RUTH
Taid, I got some flowers for you.

TAID
Oh, now they are lovely, aren't they? Hm, now maybe you should give them to Mama, I think she would really like them. What do you think?

RUTH
Yes.

TAID
Right, you give them to Mama then when she comes home. (*Ruth arranges them*) Come on, let's make a kite together before she gets back.

RUTH
How are we going to do that?

TAID
Well you just watch me. I've got everything ready in this big box. (*Taid drags a big box from the cupboard filled with paraphernalia*) We'll cut this paper to give it a tail with all the colours of the rainbow on it. These two bean sticks are for the cross pieces, like that and some brown paper to cover the lot. Good, the glue's dry. (*He tugs at the pieces previously made.*)

RUTH
Where's the string to stop it blowing away?

TAID
Here, this is special. It's stronger than the string that holds Dada's boots together. Not even a shooting star could break this! There we are, it's finished.

RUTH
Can I fly it now?

TAID
Go and find Davy, he'll show you how. (*Exit Ruth with kite*) (*Taid goes to sleep*)

MRS JONES (*Enter Mrs Jones with shopping bag. She puts the kettle on*) Are you having a cup of tea, Dad? (*No answer*) (*Banging at the door.*) What now! (*Exasperated*) Come in! (*Enter Mrs Hopkin*)

MRS HOPKIN
Sorry to trouble you again, Mrs Jones, but… I need some milk for the baby.

MRS JONES
What! Again! Here! (*She pours some milk into a jug and impatiently ushers Mrs Hopkin out of the door*)

(*Enter Ruth and Davy with kite. Ruth wakes up Taid.*)

RUTH
It doesn't fly, Taid.

TAID (*Looks at it disconsolately*)
Well, when you go to the seaside in the summer you can take it with you. It'll fly there, there's more wind there!

(*Ruth sees Mrs Jones leaning against the door, depressed, and quietly gives the flowers to Mrs Jones.*)

MRS JONES
That leg playing you up, son?

DAVY
I can't walk proper, Mam.

MRS JONES
Oh you can't, can you? I think we'll have to get a doctor, a home visit, yes? Well, not yet, tomorrow, maybe.

TAID
A home visit, it'll cost a fortune!

MRS JONES
He's very feverish, anyway, he deserves it, he's been working really hard at the Maypole.

TAID
Working hard, my foot. What have you been doing to have your mother spoil you like that?

A FEW DAYS LATER

(*Mrs Jones finishes mopping the floor and puts the bucket away prior to the arrival of Dr Ryan. She places newspapers on the damp floor to keep it clean. Mr Jones enters, his face black from working at the pit. He comes to a sudden halt and shakes his head in dismay when he sees the paper-covered floor. He hops over the gaps between the newspapers and reaches his chair and lifts the cushion.*)

MRS JONES
Dr Ryan will be here soon so don't make yourself comfortable.

MR JONES
Where's the paper? (*He lifts a sodden page off the floor*) I haven't finished reading this. (*He reads the sodden sheet*) Cor! The King's dead!

MRS JONES
What! (*She rushes over to read it*) Football! Fool. You shouldn't joke about things like that!

MR JONES (*Mr Jones sits down*)
I see you been polishing the door knocker again. It's so shiny I could see my face in it. How many tins of Brasso do you get through in a week?

MRS JONES (*She studiously ignores him.*)
Lift your feet. (*She shouts to Ruth from the parlour*) You can come in now, Ruth! (*Enter Ruth. Davy enters from the backyard, limping*)

MRS MORGAN (*Mrs Morgan enters with her large jug of milk*)
I can see your lad's not well, so I thought I'd help him. These jugs is heavy. Hello Mr Jones, just finished, have you?

(*Mr Jones mumbles and hides behind the remnants of the newspaper.*)
(*Mrs Morgan pours milk into the small jug on the table.*)

MRS JONES
The twopence is there, Mrs Morgan.

MRS MORGAN
Eh! Listen to this. Her down the road, she said to me, are your cows kept on a pasture, 'cos I want pasteurised milk, they say all the germs is killed if it's pasteurised. Ugh, she's never been right in the head since her husband was killed on the railway, it was the shock, see, never been right since. Your lad said the doctor's coming here, maybe he could take a look at my leg. I got no insurance, so it'll cost me two bob if I have to go to the surgery.

TAID (enter Taid from the parlour)
What's all the noise about? (He has seen Mrs Morgan and begins to roll one of his special cigarettes threateningly.)

MRS MORGAN
No, no, maybe not, I'm in too much of a hurry.
(*Exit Mrs Morgan.*)

MR JONES (*shocked and dismayed*)
I don't believe it! That woman… that woman could get past those fellows who guard the Crown Jewels.

MRS JONES
I don't know why Mrs Morgan feels she has to come in this house with the milk all the time. She doesn't bother going next door.

MR JONES
Maybe she likes your company.

MRS JONES (*looking through the kitchen window*)
Look at her! Racing down the path, where's her bad leg now! Why did you let her in, David?

DAVY
I didn't, she came straight after me, I couldn't stop her.

MRS JONES (*She shakes her head impatiently*)
Here! Take this bowl of water and go upstairs and give yourself a good wash before the doctor comes and be quick about it, he'll be here soon. (*Exit Davy*) Get rid of that filthy thing before the doctor comes.

TAID (*Mumbles*)
It got rid of her.

(*Bang, bang, bang on the front door*)

MRS JONES
The doctor's here. (*He enters without ceremony*) Oh hello Doctor, come in please. I'll tell David you are here. (*At the bottom of the stairs*) David!

DOCTOR
I'll just warm my hands before I examine the patient. Hello Mr Jones, how are you? It's quite cold this morning.

TAID
Oh, not too bad, Doctor. My chest is a bit tight though.

DOCTOR
Well I'm not surprised, smoking that thing. It can't be doing you any good, you know.

TAID
It's too late to worry about that now. I was down the pit for forty years, so I don't think my bit of bacca will harm me.

DOCTOR
No, maybe not.

MRS JONES
Here he is, Doctor. David, stand up straight and look at Dr Ryan!

DOCTOR
Well hello David, and how are you? Tell me what's wrong with yourself.

DAVY
It's my leg, Doctor. Here.

DOCTOR
Right, well let's have a look at you. Move your leg backwards and forwards, would you? It's very inflamed. You were right to call me, Mrs Jones.

MRS JONES
Oh, so it is serious.

DOCTOR
Well I don't think we will have to cut it off, Mrs Jones.

RUTH
Ooh! Will Davy have to have a wooden leg like Mr Williams at the Co-op?

MR JONES
Shush! No! Taid's silly remedies.

DOCTOR
Now calm down, Mr Jones. It's no use getting excited. Your father was just the same when you were a tiny baby and I brought you home in my black bag!

RUTH
What? Me, in there? Have you got a baby in there now?

DOCTOR
No, but maybe one day, one day.

MRS JONES
Get into the yard, you! (*Ruth hides behind a chair and watches*)

DOCTOR
Well that should do the trick. Your mother tells me you've been working in town, David.

DAVY
Yes, at the Maypole stores, but I am finishing there and starting at the colliery on Monday morning, in the Lamp Room.

DOCTOR
Ah, a proper job, well I hope you enjoy it. (*Unconvincingly*) Ooh, these books, do you read them or just look at the pictures? (*Smiling*) Um, I must hurry along now. Change the dressing every day, Mrs Jones, and don't hesitate to call me if it's not improving. Good day. (*Exit*)

RUTH
Why does he talk different from us, Mama?

MRS JONES
Because he's a doctor, darling.

LIGHTS DOWN

LATER

RUTH
Mama, can we have a game of shopping?

MRS JONES
Oh, all right, go and get your shopping bag.

Hello Miss Jones, and what can I get you today?

RUTH
I'll have some tea, Lipton's if you please, some soap, a tin of cocoa and a penny worth of broken biscuits.

(*Mrs Jones places these imaginary items in the child's bag whilst still ironing with the other hand*) (*Mrs Jones goes to the cupboard and from the container brings out a handful of biscuits and gives them to Ruth*)

RUTH
Thank you, Mrs Jones. Here is sixpence. I've got to go now, I've got a lot to do today. Good morning. (*She collects her kite from the sideboard*)

Exits running to backyard.

MRS JONES (*Moves to the bottom of the stairs*)
Taid! Are you all right up there? (*Exits upstairs to check on Taid and then returns to kitchen*)

(*Frantic banging at the back door*)

RUTH
Mama! Mama!

MRS JONES
Oh, what's the matter now!

RUTH (*Ruth bursts through the door and runs to Mrs Jones*)
Mama! Mama! There's a man in a big black hat chasing me!

MRS JONES
That's the man from the naughty children's home... well I did warn you!

MR JACOBS (*enter Mr Jacobs*) (*a Jewish travelling salesman, carrying a kite*) (*very apologetic*) I'm sorry, I hope I haven't frightened the little girl. Your daughter, yes?

MRS JONES (*taken aback*)
No, no, I mean yes, she is my daughter but she's a bit shy, that's all. We don't get many strangers around here, we usually take them for debt collectors until they can prove otherwise, if you know what I mean. You're not a debt...

MR JACOBS
No, no. Forgive me, let me introduce myself. My name is Jacobs, Abraham Jacobs. I am a tailor, I sell clothes, I make clothes. Yes, I am Abraham Jacobs, Tailor (*proudly*). And yourself?

MRS JONES
Jones, Mrs Jones. I'm afraid we don't want anything at the moment, thank you.

MR JACOBS
Yes, maybe, but don't be too hasty, think of the future, it will soon be autumn, then winter. I have some very nice overcoats for the winter, and inexpensive. A jacket maybe? What is your pleasure? An overcoat? (*Tentatively*)

MRS JONES
An overcoat! (*She looks at the suitcase, puzzled*)

MR JACOBS
Well, not here, right now, but in my little car, outside, my Austin 7 (*proudly*). I will bring them in. (*Exits*)

MR JONES
Will you get rid of him! And whatever you do, don't offer him a cup of tea! (*Impatiently*)

MR JACOBS (*Enter Mr Jacobs with overcoat*)
Ah, Mr Jones. Here, look! The very best, it belonged to a gentleman. A gentleman mind you, but he just passed away. This quality of merchandise would cost three guineas in Burtons, if they sold one as good as this. Three guineas, a week's wage! This is far better quality than anything you could buy in town. The best material, the finest Melton, silk lining, genteel appearance, craftsmanship in every stitch.

MR JONES
Let's have a look at it. (*He is intrigued. Mr Jones tries it on*) The buttons are too loose, it's too big!

MR JACOBS
Mrs Jones can easily pull them in. Isn't that right, Mrs Jones?

MR JONES
How much?

MR JACOBS
Twelve and six.

MR JONES
Twelve and six! We can't afford that!

MR JACOBS
I know you don't get much pay digging coals, but don't misunderstand me, I'm a working man like yourself, I didn't always have a car, I started with a bicycle. I tell you what, eleven shillings and you get six months to pay. That's only… five months at two shillings and the last months payment at one shilling. Just eleven shillings.

MR JONES
What do you think, Mam?

MRS JONES
Oh… yes, why not, you look really smart, you won't get another chance. All right Mr Jacobs, two shillings today and then two shillings when you come again.

MR JACOBS
Good, here's your card. Fill in please. (*They do the necessary*)

MRS JONES
Right, would you like a cup of tea before you go? The kettle's boiled.

MR JACOBS
Thank you, no milk, thank you. Thank you, Mrs Jones, you're very kind. You know, when I tell my mother I'm coming to North Wales, she asked me if the people here are kind to Jews. She gets worried about me. I tell her, "Mother, it's like reading the Tanakh. It's the same as your Bible, but it's the Jewish Bible, wherever you go there is a Moriah, Jerusalem, Hermon, Bethesda, (*in hushed tones*) there's even a Sodom. "That, I do not need to know," she tells me.

MRS JONES
Why is she worried about you coming to North Wales?

MR JACOBS
Ah, she's never been to North Wales, she doesn't know where North Wales is and we've lived in Manchester for twenty years. Ach, she doesn't like to leave Cheetham Hill. Nah, I tell a lie, sometimes she visits her cousin in London and sometimes she go with Beth Israel to Southport, like your chapel goes to, what's that place, Rhyl, yes, Rhyl. She's a little bit nervous you know. She prefers to stay close to Jewish people. We had to leave Russia, that's my home, Russia, well it was, but we had to leave (*dispiritedly*) because of bad men, "pogromchiks", um… troublemakers. They don't like Jewish people, they make things difficult for us, very difficult. They burn our house, all the Jew's house, throw stones at us, they even kill people. So we think, maybe it's time we go live somewhere else. Now the only Jews still there are the one sleeping in the cemetery, that's why my mother worry about me.

(He quickly gulps his tea and makes his apologies) I have to leave now, lots of calls to make. I will call again on the twenty-eighth of next month. Goodbye. (Mrs Jones accompanies him to the front door whilst Mr Jones admires his new coat. The front door slams shut.)

LIGHTS DOWN

LATER

(The Hopkin household. The room is unkempt and shabby. Ragged curtains, no carpet and a pile of clothes on the floor. Mrs Hopkin stands at a table ironing. There is banging at the front door. Enter Mr Hopkin, face black with coal dust. He slumps down into a chair and opens a bottle of stout brought from his jacket pocket)

MRS HOPKIN
Do you have to start drinking that stuff as soon as you get into the house?

MR HOPKIN (*Angrily*)
I've been soaked to the skin all night, water coming through the roof in Number two Level, sweated like a pig at the Dennis end and I'm not ready to dry out yet, so shut up and get me dinner! (*Knock at the door*) Bloody hell, who's that? (*Mrs Hopkin hesitates*) Well, go and see who it is, woman. (*She exits*) (*Mr Hopkin shouts*) if it's anybody collecting, tell them to bugger off! (*Continuing to drink from the stout bottle*) (*Mrs Hopkin re-enters*)

MR HOPKIN
Who was it then?

MRS HOPKIN
Just some old man selling stuff.

(*Knock at the front door*)

MR HOPKIN
Bloody hell, is there no peace in this house! (*Mrs Hopkin continues ironing*) Well go on woman, answer it! (*Mrs Hopkin exits and re-enters*)

MRS HOPKIN
It's the Bobby (*Mrs Hopkin enters with a policeman, Sgt Rees*)

MR HOPKIN
What the bloody hell do you want in my house?

SERGEANT REES
Keep a civil tongue in your head Hopkin, that sort of Bolshie talk won't get you anywhere. There's been some trouble at the works.

MRS HOPKIN
Do you want to sit down Constable, oh, I mean Sergeant? (*Mr Hopkin frowns as she pulls a chair from under the table. It is piled with washing et cetera. The sergeant winces at the sight of it*)

MR HOPKIN
Trouble, what do you mean trouble, what are you talking about, man? And make sure you keep a civil tongue in your head too, this is my house!

SERGEANT REES (*impatiently*)
I have to speak to your son John.

MR HOPKIN
What about?

SERGEANT REES
Never you mind, I want to see him first. Is he at home? I know he's not at work, I've checked.

MR HOPKIN
Oh, you have, have you, very bloody efficient.

MRS HOPKIN (*Nervously*)
What's it about, Sergeant?

SERGEANT REES (*He changes his tone as he speaks to Mrs Hopkin*)
A gold box has gone missing from one of the engine houses, Mrs Hopkin. A party of gentlemen were visiting the colliery on a tour of inspection, when a small gold snuff box belonging to one of them went missing…

MR HOPKIN
A gold box! And you think our John took it I suppose! A gold box! Why him? There's a hundred men go past that block every day!

SERGEANT REES
Look, Mr Hopkin, I have to address my questions to the boy. Is he here or isn't he? And if he isn't, where is he?

MRS HOPKIN
Still in bed.

MR HOPKIN
Still in bed! The lazy bugger, I'll give him still in bed! (*Mr Hopkin walks over to the stairs and shouts up*) When are you getting up lad, you've missed one shift already this week. Your wages won't be worth picking up! Don't think I'm going to feed you!

MRS HOPKIN
Don't make so much noise, you'll wake the baby. (*Mrs Hopkin goes upstairs to rouse the boy*) (*the Sergeant waits until Mrs Hopkin disappears*)

SERGEANT REES
I know you of old, Hopkin, are you bringing up your son the same way?

MR HOPKIN
I don't know what you're talking about.

SERGEANT REES
You know very well what I'm talking about, pinching coal off the sidings.

MR HOPKIN
It was our coal, we dug it, anyway you got no charges against me!

SERGEANT REES
You were lucky that time, you can run fast, I'll say that for you!

(*Enter Mrs Hopkin and John*) (*Mr Hopkin alerts John to the accusation*)

MR HOPKIN
Huh! A gold box, you say. He wouldn't know the difference between a gold box and a brass candlestick. You'd be better telling the silly bugger that lost it not to carry gold boxes about the place, instead of barging into people's homes asking stupid questions.

SERGEANT REES
Don't tell me how to do my job, Hopkin. Are you John Edward Hopkin?

MR HOPKIN
No, he's Douglas Fairbanks, who the bloody hell do you think he is!

SERGEANT REES
I would ask you not to interrupt, Mr Hopkin, your son could be in serious trouble. Right, I'll start again, are you John Edward Hopkin?

JOHN
Yes.

SERGEANT REES
Where were you at about a quarter past two yesterday afternoon?

JOHN
I was on the yard, I just finished my shift.

SERGEANT REES
Where on the yard?

JOHN
Well, just crossing over to the gate... so I could go home.

SERGEANT REES
Were you in the vicinity of the engine house?

JOHN
In the what?

SERGEANT REES
In the vic… In the same area as the engine house?

JOHN
No.

SERGEANT REES
You were seen by the engine house, we have a number of witnesses to that so it's no use you trying to deny it. (*John hesitates*) Come on, speak up lad! Were you by the engine house yesterday afternoon? Well, what are you looking so guilty for, have you got something to hide?

JOHN
No, it's just that I've been told to keep away from the engine house by the pithead foreman.

SERGEANT REES
So what were you doing there when you've been told to keep away?

JOHN
I went to see Bert Rowlands the engineman. He keeps ponies on a field near here, I wanted to scrounge some turnips off him to give to the ponies down the pit. I chop them up into little pieces, they love them.

SERGEANT REES
I've got to ask you some questions about a very expensive item that has gone missing at the works. It's a small box about this big (3"x2") gold in colour. Do you have such a thing in your possession?

JOHN
No.

SERGEANT REES
It's got a lid covered in coloured glass that makes up a picture of a big church like the one in town. Well?

JOHN
No.

SERGEANT REES
It's been damaged slightly (*turning to Mrs Hopkin*), according to the owner this was done during the war when he was in France. There's some French writing on it.

MR HOPKIN (*very impatiently*)
He's told you. NO!

SERGEANT REES

Any more interruptions from you and I'll be taking the both of you down to the Station! Do you know that finding other people's property and keeping it for yourself is a criminal offence?

JOHN
No.

MR HOPKIN
This gentleman (*sarcastically*) that's lost this precious box (*sarcastically*), did you ask him how he got it in the first place? Probably picked it up from some bombed out mansion in France. (*emphatically*) Did you tell him (*with emphasis*) that finding other people's property and keeping it for yourself is a criminal offence?

SERGEANT REES
Watch what you're saying Hopkin, you could end up in court for slander! I could carry out a search, you know. (*He winces at the prospect*)

MR HOPKIN
Not without a warrant you can't! Now if you've finished, I want my dinner, I just done a proper job, so bugger off and make a nuisance of yourself somewhere else.

SERGEANT REES
You haven't heard the last of this. Thank you for your help, Mrs Hopkin. (*Exits with Mrs Hopkin*)

MRS HOPKIN
I'll see you to the door, Sergeant.

MR HOPKIN
You will not, you're not his bloody skivvy, sit down!

SERGEANT REES (*Sergeant exits and turns by the door*)
Another thing. There have been reports of pilfering from the coal bunkers.

MR HOPKIN
What's that got to do with me?

SERGEANT REES
I just thought I'd let you know the management is aware of what's going on.

MR HOPKIN
Whoever took it, they're entitled to it, they dug it out so they're entitled to a bit of extra coal!

SERGEANT REES
That coal is owned by the company.

MR HOPKIN
Maybe, but they don't own me, there's no harm in it!

SERGEANT REES
Try telling that to the magistrates, because that's where you're going to end up! I'll see to that! (*Exit*)

MR HOPKIN (*He watches the sergeant exit the front door*)
Listen to him, 'Thank you for your help, Mrs Hopkin'. (*Sarcastically.*) She's treating him like royalty! What you being so nice to him for? The big-headed sod! He'd arrest you for breathing if he could get away with it. Well, do you know anything about this bloody box he's on about?

JOHN
No.

MR HOPKIN
You bloody liar. (*He hits John across the head*) Did you pinch it or what?

JOHN
No, Dad, I found it on the path by the office.

MR HOPKIN
Where is it now?

JOHN
I threw it away. (*Mr Hopkin raises his hands to hit John again*) I did, I threw it in the river when I heard them talking about it in the office. I got scared and threw it away. That's why I didn't go to work today, I was scared.

MR HOPKIN
You bloody fool! We could have got some money for that! (*Mr Hopkin slumps back into his chair and continues drinking*) (*Silence*) (*He stares at John in disbelief*) What are you doing?

JOHN
Just filling in the holes with a bit of cardboard. (*John cuts a piece of cardboard from an oxo box and stuffs it into his boots to block the holes in the soles*)

MR HOPKIN
Bloody cardboard! What a life.

MRS HOPKIN
Leave the lad alone, he's doing his best. His feet were blue with cold last night. (*A knock at the back door*)

MR HOPKIN
Bloody hell, what now! Oh, it's you. (*He bangs the arm of the chair*)
(*A man peers around the door*)

BILLY WILLIAMS
All right to come in? I saw Sergeant Rees leaving the front door. I been waiting round the corner till he left. What did the old sod want?

MR HOPKIN
Ah, just a bit of bother with our John, nothing important. (*To Mrs Hopkin*) Go and see to the baby, I heard her squawking a minute ago. (*Mrs Hopkin leaves*) He said they was watching the coal staithes (*he indicates with this thumb to the departed policeman*) (*speaking to John*) You haven't been down there, have you?

JOHN (*indignantly*)
No!

MR HOPKIN
Well, keep away from there, don't give them an excuse to come after you. (*To Billy Williams*) Have you seen the watchman nosing down by the sidings?

BILLY WILLIAMS
Nah, he's stuck in his cabin most times reading his Bible, he only steps outside for a pee.

MR HOPKIN
You go down there one of these nights and chuck some big lumps off the tops of them wagons what's on the end of the line by the buffers, we could do with some more coal now the cold nights is here. Make sure they roll down the bank so they end up in the brambles, nobody will see them there and I can pick them up on my way home from the pub. (*Mrs Hopkin re-enters*) (*They stop speaking*)

MRS HOPKIN
She's got a bad cough and I haven't got money for medicine. I didn't have money for the rent man, neither.

MR HOPKIN
No money, what you talking about woman, I put it on the mantelpiece on payday!

MRS HOPKIN
Well it didn't stay there long, it wasn't there when I went for it to pay the rent man.

MR HOPKIN (*Mr Hopkin jumps up and searches the mantelpiece for the missing money*)
Oh! (*He remembers. He pulls coins out of his pockets and gives them to Mrs Hopkin. She counts it.*)

MRS HOPKIN
What am I going to do with this, there's not enough, two shillings!
(*Mr Hopkin is getting angry*)

BILLY WILLIAMS (*wanting to avoid the argument between the Hopkin's*) (*to Hopkin*)
Tom! I think it's time… I think I'll go now. I'm off to the Black Lion. Make sure you bring that stuff I asked you for.

MR HOPKIN (*Hopkin acknowledges*)
Will do!

JOHN (*incredulously*)

The Black Lion again! (*He looks at the time*) It's not opening time yet. Haven't you got a job yet?

BILLY WILLIAMS
There's no work about, Johnny bach, can't get a job for love or money. (*Mock serious*)

JOHN
Sammy Owens needs a haulier at the pit, why don't you try him for a job?

BILLY WILLIAMS
Humph. The only way you'll get me underground is when I'm dead!

JOHN
I don't know how you get away with it.

BILLY
It's me old war wound. (*cough cough*) See?

JOHN
You wasn't in the bloody war, you told me yourself! I just don't know how…

MR HOPKIN (mockingly)
He's got a friend down at the Labour exchange, old Mr Eatherington, very compassionate, very understanding he is.

JOHN
Very bloody senile if you ask me. Daft bugger!

MR HOPKIN
Oh, he's not daft, he's got his eye on Billy's sister.

JOHN
Megan? But she's got a face like a slapped arse!

BILLY
Hoi, watch it, that's my sister you're talking about.

MR HOPKIN
Well when you get old like Eatherington, it's a case of any port in a storm. Ha ha!

BILLY WILLIAMS (*To John*) (*All the time, Mrs Hopkin looks on sullenly*)
And you, you just remember to bring that stuff, that's all. (*He wags his finger at Harry and makes a hasty exit by the back door*)

MR HOPKIN
What do you think you're doing, talking like that in front of Billy Williams, showing me up, it'll be all around the Black Lion by closing time.

MRS HOPKIN
They already know.

(*Mr Hopkin hits her*)

JOHN
Dad … Dad, no! (*Mr Hopkin goes to hit her again. He lets her fall to the floor. John helps her. Mr Hopkin exits, banging the door behind him*) Don't worry about the money, Mam, I'll get it for you. I'll work overtime.

(*Jenny, the eldest daughter, appears at the bottom of the stairs*)

MRS HOPKIN
Thank you, son.

(*A baby wails plaintively*)
Mama!

MRS HOPKIN
I'll have to go and see to the baby. (*Exit, upstairs*)

(*Exit John, slowly and depressed*) (*Jenny silently watches from the bottom of the stairs*)

CURTAINS

LATER

(*Outside the Black Lion public house, Davy is limping, bike in tow*)

JOHN (*John, shoulders hunched, despondent, perks up on seeing Davy*)
Hoi! Hopalong Cassidy, what you doing wearing that apron, you still an errand boy? I thought you said you was leaving.

DAVY
I am, I am. I'm starting in the Lamp Room Monday morning.

JOHN
About time you got a proper job.

DAVY
I'm not a collier yet!

JOHN
No! But you soon will be and in a few months you'll be underground. Hey! What's the matter with your leg, you're hobbling along like old Mr Williams at the Co-op. (*He mimics Davy's limp*) "The mean buggers won't even give me two shillings war pension." (*Mimicking Mr Williams*)

DAVY
I got a boil. I got some ointment from the doctor but it still hurts. Hey… John… How old are you?

JOHN
How old? What do you want to know that for?

DAVY
Oh, it's just that you look younger than the other lads on your shift, you don't look as old as them. When was you born?

JOHN (*irritated*)
I don't know, maybe me dad made me older so as he could get me working in the pit, a bit like those kids what fiddle their age so they can get into the army. Hey, who's that funny looking bugger I saw outside your house?

DAVY
He sells stuff to man. He's Jewish, or something.

JOHN
Ah, I thought he was something like that. They'll get it when the revolution comes, Davy. Me Dad says they're in league with the bosses.

DAVY
But he can't be in league with the bosses, John, he's only selling clothes and most of them are second-hand. He's not a boss.

JOHN
He's got a CAR, hasn't he? (*Emphatically*) Hey, Davy, look at this! (*He produces a box from his jacket pocket*)

DAVY
Wow! What is it?

JOHN
Smart, innit? It's a box for baccy and stuff. Look at all coloured bits, they're glass or something. It's made from real gold or something. You can have it.

DAVY (incredulous)
No!

JOHN
Yes, go on, it's for you, take it.

DAVY
Oh, John, thanks!

JOHN
But don't tell anybody!

DAVY
It's got some writing on it. Where did you get it, John?

JOHN
Um… One of me uncles gave it to me. He was in France in the war. He got it when he was
out there, like a souvenir I suppose, but keep it secret.

DAVY
I will, I will. Cor, it's the best thing I've ever had, thanks John. I've never had anything as
nice as this before. (*He grips it tightly and puts it in his pocket*)

JOHN
Come on, Davy, I'm starving, I want my tea. Even if it is only bread and dripping. (He puts
his arm round Davy's shoulder and they exit, singing)
      "Down the pit we want to go,
      Away from school and all its woe!
      Working hard as a collier's butty
      Makes us all so very happy!
      Did you ever see, did you ever see, did you ever see such a funny thing before!"
(*From Tosher Bailey's Engine song*)

DAVY (*limping*)
Hoi! Wait for me!

LATER

(*Lights down… Lights up. Dark, late evening about 10:30 PM, same place outside the Black
Lion*) (*the sound of chatter and laughter comes from the pub. Alongside the pub there is a
high brick wall with a door set into it. There is a hazy glow from a distant street lamp.
Sergeant Rees and Constable Price are watching from the shadows. There have been reports
of after-hours drinking and the sergeant is ready to pounce and make an arrest.*)

REES
What time do you make it? (*They synchronise watches*)

PRICE
Half past ten.

REES
It's too early to go in and catch them drinking after hours. They've got another ten minutes
yet. You carry on with your rounds but don't make yourself obvious. And make sure you're
back here when I'm ready to go in. (*Exit Constable Price*) I'll catch the buggers this time!

(*Time passes. A figure appears out of the darkness carrying a sack and startles the
unprepared Sergeant who moves further back into the shadows. The figure opens the yard
door and enters the backyard of the pub. Sgt Rees guesses that it is Hopkin carrying an illicit
sack of coal. He tries to dash over and catch Hopkin but the door slams in his face and the
door bolt clangs. He rattles the door but it is bolted tight. There is the sound of scuffling on a
back wall and the sound of hobnailed boots clattering down a back alley. Sgt Rees withdraws
to the shadows cursing. Revellers come and go. A little girl enters.*)

SERGEANT REES
What are you doing out at this time of night, you should be in bed!

GIRL
I'm by myself, my mam and dad have gone out and they're not back yet.

SERGEANT REES
You're Jim Hopkin's girl, aren't you?

GIRL
Yes

SERGEANT REES
I've got a feeling your father's back home by now so he'll be wondering where you are, so get going. (*She doesn't move*) Get going! (*Angry*) Make sure you lock the door after you.

GIRL
I can't do that, Dad said not to.

SERGEANT REES
Why?

GIRL
I don't know, he broke it last time and he shouted at me.

SERGEANT REES (*Rees shakes his head, perplexed*)
Get going! (*Exit girl*) (*Exit Sgt Rees to check the back wall. He re-enters and takes his position in the shadows*) (*Constable Price arrives*) I wish you'd have been here five minutes ago, that bloody Hopkin went in there with a sack of coal. I couldn't catch him, too quick, this damn knee of mine slowed me down.

CONSTABLE PRICE
How did you know it was Hopkin, it's proper dark in there, Sarge.

SERGEANT REES
It was somebody up to no good, normal people don't leave a pub by clambering over a garden wall and running down the street. He knocked half a dozen bricks off the top in his hurry to get away. Anyway I'd know Hopkin anywhere, that coughing and wheezing, I could recognise him a mile off. Hello, who's this coming now, he's carrying a sack as well. I don't believe it, he's come back, the nerve of the man, this could be our lucky night! Come on! Don't move Hopkin or I swear I'll break your bloody arm! (*They catch hold of the man and shine a torch in his face*) Bloody hell, it's Billy Williams, what are you doing here? What's in this sack?

BILLY (*Sardonically*)
Rabbits.

SGT REES
Rabbits! Very funny. Well rabbits come out of a top hat, not out of a sack. (*He upturns the sack and rabbits fall to the ground*)

BILLY
Rabbits, see?

SGT REES
What's your game, Williams?

BILLY
I'm going to hang them up in the cold room at the back of the pub. It's a little arrangement I got with Mr Perrin the landlord, he gets a few rabbits and I get a few pints after closing time. (*Emphatically*) It's a private invitation so it's not against the law!

REES
Ugh! Let him go.

(*Williams tries the yard door but it is bolted. He drops the sack and enters the pub door whilst the two policemen look on disconsolately*) Well it's a waste of time stopping here now, the whole pub will know we're waiting for them. I'm going back to the station, I'll have to write a report on tonight's little fiasco. The Superintendent will be pleased!

PRICE
Hey Sarge, we could get Williams for poaching.

SGT REES
Poaching?

CONSTABLE PRICE
Yes! How do you think he got those rabbits!

SGT REES
Poaching! I've got better things to do. I'm not the Duke's gamekeeper!

CONSTABLE PRICE
How about trespassing?

SGT REES
Where exactly? It's not Billy Williams I want, it's that bloody Hopkin! You carry on with your rounds. Go this way (*he points in the opposite direction to the pub*) Don't let them see you passing, they'll all have their noses stuck to the window watching you, laughing!

CONSTABLE PRICE
Goodness me, standing outside the pub trying to catch a few boozers.

SGT REES
Not good enough for you?

CONSTABLE PRICE
Well, I got my future to think about Sarge, I don't want to be stuck here for the rest of my life. I fancy having a go with the Met. or the City.

SGT REES
Oh, you been reading their recruitment posters, have you?

CONSTABLE PRICE
Yes of course, they seem to have a good opinion of us up here otherwise why would they be pasting their posters everywhere? They must trust us.

SGT REES
Or maybe they think we're too dozy to get involved with the crooks they get down there, if you know what I mean.

CONSTABLE PRICE (*Shocked*)
Humph! Or too honest! I wouldn't be involved in any of that sort of thing, Sarge.

SGT REES
No, indeed (*he rolls his eyes*) not.

CONSTABLE PRICE
See you later, Sarge.

SGT REES
Oh, Hopkin's little girl is out wandering the streets. Watch out for her, make sure she gets home safely. (*The bolt on the back yard door bangs open and Billy Williams retrieves his sack of rabbits and re-enters the yard and bangs the bolt shut*)

BILLY (*sarcastically*)
Goodnight, Sergeant.

(*Exit Sergeant Rees, grumbling*)

LATER THAT EVENING. THE JONES HOUSE
(*Ruth is asleep on a chair.*)

MRS JONES (*Faint knocking at the door*)
Was that the door? (*Knock, knock*) That's the door again. Well don't rush at once, will you?

MR JONES
Go and look who's at the door for your Mam.

MRS JONES
Indeed not at this time of night. (*She stares at Mr Jones*)

MR JONES
All right, all right, I'll go! It's Jenny. She says she's cold. (*Jenny and Mr Jones enter.*)

MRS JONES
Hello, Jenny. What's the matter, Cariad? The poor girl's starving. Come and sit by the fire. Have a cup of cocoa, darling. What are you doing out at this time of night? Where's your Mam?

JENNY
She's gone with Dad to visit a friend. They haven't come back yet and John's in work. I'm afraid of the dark but I can't get the gas on. Dad said I was to go to bed when it got dark but I don't like going upstairs in the dark, 'cause I'm afraid of it.

MRS JONES
Oh dear. Well you sit there and drink your cocoa. (*Loud knock knock*) I'm sure that will be your Mam. Davy! The door! (*Mr Jones rises from his chair and sits back down again.*) (*Exit Davy to front door and he re-enters with Mr Hopkin.*)

DAVY
It's Mr Hopkin, Mam.

MR HOPKIN
So there you are, you little madam. What do you think you're doing here, worrying Mrs Jones. I'm sorry, Mrs Jones. I told you to go to bed if we wasn't back. (*Drunkenly*)

JENNY
You said you was only going to be half an hour.

MR HOPKIN
Don't you – (*He raises his hand as if to strike Jenny*) Come here. (*He grabs Jenny's hand.*)

JENNY
You're squeezing my hand too tight!

MR HOPKIN
I'll belt you in a minute if you don't stop crying. You wait till I get you home.

JENNY
I'm not going home. I'm going to run away.

MR HOPKIN
You'll what? Run away? Hah! You'd trip over your own feet. Kids! They'd drive you to Denbigh, wouldn't they! I hope she hasn't been too much trouble for you, Mrs Jones.

MRS JONES
No, no.

MR HOPKIN
Come on you! (*He pulls Jenny towards the door*) (*Exit*)

MRS JONES
Did you smell his breath? He stinks of beer. Oh, I'd like to slap his face for him. (*Mr Hopkin and Jenny exit and slam the door*) (*Ruth wakes up*)

RUTH
Mama! Mama! Is someone hurt, Mama?

MRS JONES
No, darling. (*Speaking to Mr Jones under her breath*) No, not yet, but there soon will be.

DAVY
Mam, when are we going to leave here?

MRS JONES
It won't be long now, we'll have our new house soon enough, but it's not only here that
there's trouble (*she points next door*) you know. Look at the time! You two should have been
in bed hours ago, come on, up the wooden hills.
(*Noises of banging and shouting from next door*)

MR JONES
Yes, Davy! Work for you on Monday! You'll need all your energy! And keep your noise
down. Don't disturb Taid!

LIGHTS DOWN

SUNDAY. THE BACK KITCHEN.
(*Mrs Jones, Bible in hand, and Ruth are ready for chapel*)

MR JONES
We'll have to kit you out ready for tomorrow and remember, we've got to be ready to leave
by half past five so… You're going to do some proper work for a change.

DAVY (*Davy rolls his eyes impatiently*)
Yes, Dad.

MRS JONES
Oh, does he have to go underground? Let him stay in the Lamproom.

MR JONES
Be quiet woman, he's starting tomorrow, we've been through all this before, like I was saying
we haven't got time to waste. Get out of those clothes and try these on (*empties a kit bag of
old clothes*) They're good enough for underground. You don't need a collar and tie, it's not
the Lamproom.

DAVY
Yes, Dad. (*He rolls his eyes again*) Will I be working with you and Uncle Albert?

MR JONES
I don't know, wait and see.

DAVY (*he picks up some clothes*)
They're awfully smelly, Dad.

MR JONES
Well you had better get used to it, hadn't you, it's a lot worse down the pit!

MRS JONES
Do you have to be so sharp with the lad?

MR JONES
He's got to learn fast, it's no use mollycoddling him.

MRS JONES
Try this jacket on for size. (*Davy puts on the jacket, it's much too long*) It's a bit long but it will do for work, I'll sew the sleeves up when I get the chance. *(She hangs the jacket on the back of the chair)*

MR JONES (*He takes hold of Davy by the arm*)
Now remember, when you start underground you're not a schoolkid, you got to be obedient and brave. Now what that means is, when you're told to do something you do it and being brave is not crying to me or your Mam when you get a clout for not doing what you was told to do. Do you understand me? …But if anybody lays a hand on you… well they'll have me to deal with. (*To Mrs Jones*) There's a few down there too handy with their fists, I've seen them. (*He sits down and reads the newspaper*)

MRS JONES
Well that's as maybe but we are ready to go now. (*Mrs Jones and Ruth in their Sunday best*)

MR JONES
Well go!

MRS JONES
Dew, you're a heathen! What sort of example are you showing the children. (*He hides behind his paper*) (*she storms out of the house with Ruth in tow, slamming the door behind her*)

MR JONES
Has she gone! Right, I'm off, when she comes back tell her I've gone for a walk across the fields. (*Exit back door. John Hopkin stands at the door.*) Bloody hell you timed it right. Come in. (*Exit Mr Jones*)

DAVY
Oh, it's you!

JOHN
Don't worry, I saw your Mam… Mrs Jones disappearing round the corner, Chapel I suppose. (*He sits down and lounges on the chair*) Ready for tomorrow, the big day doing a proper job!

DAVY
Oh bloody hell, I wish people would stop going on about it.

JOHN
I got some proper fags. Woodbines! (*He lights one up for Davy and one for himself.*) (*They start smoking*) I'm glad that sister of yours isn't here, proper little tell-tale. Got some tea left, had to leave in a hurry, me Mam and Dad are at it again. Where's the milk?

DAVY
No milk till tomorrow. (*The front door rattles*) Oh bloody hell, is that me Mam! (*They both hide their cigarettes. One in the pocket of the jacket hanging on the chair*)

MRS JONES (*Mrs Jones enters and stares*)
What are you doing here on Sunday? (*She picks up a book*) You've got to get up early tomorrow, so no running around!

JOHN
Don't worry, Mrs Jones, I'll look after him.

MRS JONES
And see if Taid wants anything. (*Exit*)

JOHN (*relieved*)
Bloody hell, that was close, I think I'll go, I don't want her to catch me here again. See you tomorrow. (*Exit*)

CURTAIN

THE COLLIERY YARD, THE FOLLOWING MORNING

(The dawn rises over the colliery. Enter Mr Jones, Davy and John)

JOHN
See you in the lamproom, Davy, see you, Mr Jones. (*Exit John*)

MR JONES (*He points at the dawn sky*)
Look at that Davy, lovely isn't it, beautiful even. You know, it's a strange thing, beauty. Why does it exist? What's the point of it?

DAVY
How do you mean, Dad?

MR JONES
Well, we don't need it, beauty I mean. Things like birds singing and flowers, the sunrise, we don't need it like we need food and clothes and shelter. But there it is. Look at those stars, Davy. Scientists say that the light started out from them thousands of years ago and it's only just reached us! It's as if some great charity has put it there just for our enjoyment. Yes, they shine down on all of us, Davy, the rich and their big houses and on us going to work in the bloody pit.

DAVY
Well, yes Dad, it's God.

MR JONES
Mam told you that I suppose. (*Said with disdain but without Davy realising it*) Humph! (*Not convinced*) Look! There's a thrush. (*He stops and stares at a bird perched on a nearby roof*) "So little cause for carolings of such ecstatic sound. (*He quotes from 'The Darkling Thrush*)

DAVY
What's that, Dad?

MR JONES
From a poem I learned in the war. I had a lot of time on my hands. I did a lot of reading, there was always a book or magazine being passed around. How do, Jack. Nice day for it!

JACK
What are you so cheerful about?

MR JONES
Oh come on Jack. The sun is shining, the sky is blue, the birds is all singing.

JACK
Humph! They's not singing where we're going, are they! (*He picks up a stone and throws it at the bird.*) It's got the whole bloody sky for itself, I've got the three-foot seam this morning. (*Davy and Mr Jones look at each other and shrug.*)

MR JONES
Come here Davy, I want to show you something. See them ropes lying along there? (*They looked down into a concrete channel - the stage apron.*) They is slack at the moment but when the engine starts pulling on them they shoot up as rigid as iron bars! (*The cables start to move and Dad and Davy step back.*) See! There's a lot of them underground, so keep off them or they will have your leg off! Come on, let's collect our lamps.
(*Davy moves off first, but his father catches him by the shoulder and speaks sternly to him*) Now you've been told about your lamp, look after it, it could save your life one day, and don't let the flame go out, it's black down there, blacker than any night you've ever seen! So dark you can feel it. (*He jabs the air and draws his hands down over his face*) (*A squawking flock of geese fly overhead casting a shadow*) Look at them Davy, off to pastures new, they can fly away but what about us, eh?

DAVY
I don't know, Dad.

MR JONES
I'll tell you what about us, we're going to be late if we don't get a move on, come on. (*Exiting in a hurry*)

MR JONES
We got to check into the lamproom first and then Mr Hughes the Overman will tell you what to do. Now do what you're told and keep your wits about you 'cause you can get hurt, all right.

(The miners form a queue in the lamproom exchanging their tallies for their lamps and are checked by the Overman to ensure they are not carrying 'contraband' such as tobacco or matches, which is illegal.)

OVERMAN
You know I got to check you, I got to check for what we call is contraband, fags and matches and suchlike, you know the score, you seen me doing it often enough. (*He pats Davy*) Hello, what's this! A fag!

DAVY
I don't know!

OVERMAN
Cigarettes! Matches! (*The Overman finds more in Davy's pocket. He steps back, aghast*)

MR JONES
What the bloody hell you doing with those Davy!

DAVY
I dun'no! I dun'no!

OVERMAN
This is a very serious offence my lad!

DAVY
But they're not mine!

OVERMAN
Well what are they doing in your pocket then.

DAVY
Someone must have put them there, somebody must have left them there. It's not my jacket really, is it Dad?

MR JONES
No, no. It's my old jacket, I must have left them in the pocket when I finished with it. Weeks ago, yes… Look Mister Hughes this is a genuine mistake, the lad doesn't even smoke.

OVERMAN
Well, okay, seeing as he's your lad, but don't let it happen again, do you hear?

MR JONES
Yes, of course. Thank you, Mr Hughes. (*He drags Davy to one side*) What the hell you playing at! Your first day and you nearly get us the sack!

DAVY
Sorry, Dad. I didn't know about them, honest!

MR JONES
Jesus Christ, don't do anything else wrong today or you'll be feeling the back of my hand. We'll talk about this when we get home tonight. Come on, let's get over to the cage.

1st MINER
What you doing sending him down here? This is no life for a boy.

2nd MINER
Nor a bloody horse, neither!

MR JONES
He's got to earn a living, hasn't he!

2nd MINER
Yes, but not in a place like this.

MR JONES
You let me worry about that!

MINER
You was always a hard man, Arthur bach! Boy. (*A miner whispers in Davy's ear*) It's a thousand feet straight down. (*He points downwards*) But you'll hit the bottom soon enough. In about five seconds, ha ha. So hold on to your stomach!

MR JONES (*As walking into the cage at the pithead*)
When we start going down, mind you close your eyes now, stop the dust getting in them. And hold tight! (*Bells ring, cables whirr, cage descends*) (*John and Davy stagger out of the cage, arm in arm, laughing nervously*)

MR JONES (*At the pit bottom*)
Well done, Davy, you redeemed yourself. Some of the boys on their first trip down, they got to be pushed into the cage as stiff as a board. Anyway, this is what we call the pit bottom. Just you wait here while I find out what's happening to you. (*He walks over to an official*)

FOREMAN
Hoi you two, this isn't a playground!

1st MINER
You should tell the engineman to go easy on the brakes, my teeth is still rattling!

2nd MINER
No wonder! They never fitted proper since you bought them second-hand off old Mrs Griffiths before she buried her husband!

1st MINER
Well they was no use where he was going!

3rd MINER
You getting too old, Jacko!

1st MINER
Aye, maybe, but there's a new lad here, first time down. It wouldn't do him no harm to set us down easy like, until the lad gets used to it.

MINER
How you feeling, son?

DAVY
I'm okay, thanks.

MINER (*Sympathetic collier whispers in Davy's ear*)
First time down, was it?

DAVY
Yes.

MINER
Make it your last. (*Exit*)

JOHN
How does it feel, hanging at the end of a rope, Davy, now you know what Crippen felt like!

MINER
Was you nervous coming down?

DAVY (*Unconvincingly*)
No, no, I wasn't nervous.

1st MINER (*Sarcastically*)
Are you sure?

2nd MINER
He'll get used to it!

DAVY
No, no, I didn't mind at all. It was quite cosy in that cage, everyone squashed together like that. No, it was okay, as long as them ropes don't give way!

JOHN (*He puts his arm around Davy's shoulder*)
Shush Davy! Don't joke about ropes breaking. We never talk about such things down here. It's bad luck! (*Holding each other surreptitiously so that the foreman does not see them. They laugh nervously*)

MR JONES (*Mr Jones returns from the Foreman*)
We've got to go to the far end of the shaft, it's a long walk so we need to get going. Mr Evans is the boss down there, he'll tell you what work you will be doing when we get there! Come on, let's get a move on, we can't afford to stand here talking. (*Exit*) if you ever have to go back to the pit bottom, you know, where the cage sets down, follow the OUT signs. See there. (*He points to a large OUT sign*) if you can't find one, feel for the wind on your back and follow it. If you feel the wind on your face you going the wrong way! (*Re-enter, continuing*

their long walk to the coalface) Now you know gas is very dangerous Davy so we have to check to see if any is hanging around. Up in the roof is the worst place for it, it gets trapped in all the holes and cavities up there, (*he points to the roof*) so this is what we do, turn down your flame and if it flares up again… you know there's gas so tell one of the older men. That's okay, see, cos nothing happened to your flame, right, I'll tell you more about the gas when I have more time, we got to push on.

DAVY
Hoi Dad, is that rock safe? (*He points upwards*)

MR JONES
'Course it is, son, Joshua and all his trumpets couldn't bring that down, it's been there for years. It would need an earthquake to bring that down and we don't have earthquakes in Wales, do we? Come on. Don't you lose sight of me now, it'll be getting lower pretty soon so be careful you don't bang your head!

DAVY
How far we got to go now, Dad?

MR JONES
A good mile yet.

DAVY
A mile!

MR JONES
You're not tired already, are you?

DAVY
No, no, but we'll be back home again at this rate!

MR JONES
Only kidding. About 200 yards, that's all! Hoi, let's stop a minute. Tell me what colour that flame is.

DAVY
Sort of red, like one of those oranges I had for Christmas once.

MR JONES
Reddish-orange, that's right. That means the area is safe but when it starts turning yellow like up here (*holds the lamp near the roof*) you got to start being a bit careful cause there's gas around, well up there anyway, do you understand, and if the flame turns blue and white, well let's hope that never happens, eh! Hoi! Stand in these here manholes when a tub comes through. (*A tub of coal rumbles past noisily.*)

MR JONES (*Davy gets too close to his father*)
Step back lad, have about six feet between you and the man in front.

MINER
Heads!

MR JONES
The thing is, we keep about six feet apart so that if there's a roof fall we won't all be buried. There will be someone left to dig us out. Right!

MINER
Heads!

MR JONES
And shout 'Heads!' when we come to a low beam like this one. Bang your head on those a couple of times and you'll think you've done ten rounds with Joe Louis! And another thing, if you feels a stone drop on your head or your back, just jump out of the way quick as it might mean there's a bigger one following it, better safe than sorry isn't it! There's Mr Evans, he's the boss. (*He shouts*) Mr Evans!

MR EVANS (*Mr Evans comes over*)
You're the new lad, are you?

DAVY
Yes.

MR EVANS
Your father says you are a clever lad, can be trusted to do a good job. Well, we'll see. I hope you're sharper than the last one they sent down here, he couldn't tie his own bootlaces.

MR JONES
He's better than that! I'll just have a few words with him before I go to my place. (*He pulls Davy aside and whispers*) Now listen to me, remember what I told you, the men like to play tricks on new boys, okay? They'll ask you to run daft errands for them like go and get the rubber wedge and the key to the main gate. Well you got to ignore them, okay... He's ready Mr Evans, I've finished, see you later, son. (*He puts his hand on Davy's shoulder*) (*Mr Evans and Davy exit. Their lamp lights disappear into the distant tunnel as Mr Jones watches intently*)

MR EVANS
Right lad, see these doors, you got to keep them closed, understand, but when a tub comes along you got to open them, like this, see, so that the tub can carry on along this 'ere railway. When the tub has gone through you close the doors again, right? It's all about ventilation, see. Keeping the doors closed means we get good ventilation and we get fresh air into all the workings, well some of them anyway. Right, any questions? No? Well I'll come back later to see how you're getting on, and don't let me catch you sleeping. (*Exit*)

MINER (*Miner passing by*) Hoi, Albert, are you dreaming?

MR JONES
It's my lad. When I watched his lamp disappearing down the tunnel I was so sick, I wished he'd stayed at the Maypole Stores. If anything happens to him his mother will curse me. (*Exit together*)

(*Davy sits down by the door to await the first tub*) (*A tub rattles along in the distance*) (*Light to total blackout*) (*A tub crashes into the door*)

LATER

MINER
Come on, break time. (*Two or three miners pass by on their way to the resting place at the junction of two shafts.*) How you liking it down here anyway?

DAVY
Oh, I'm alright.

MINER
Bit different from the Lamproom, isn't it. (*Bang!!!*) (*Miner pays no attention, but Davy jumps*)

DAVY
What's that?

SARCASTIC MINER
Ha ha. That made you jump, didn't it. Didn't anyone warn you? They are blasting a new face just along the heading, makes your ears ring a bit, doesn't it. Ha ha. Do you still like it down here? You'll get used to it. (*Another bang, Davy jumps again*) Ha ha, had enough already? Well there's one good thing about this job, you'll always have a roof over your head, ha ha. (*They arrive at the junction and sits down to drink their tea.*)

MINER (*speaking to Davy*)
Keep a good strap on that snappin tin, the mice down here have got teeth like tin openers.

2nd MINER
Aye, they can take the lid off a can of beans.

MINER
Aye, but they couldn't get inside, they all got hunchbacks.

DAVY
What do you mean, hunchbacks?

2nd MINER
Hunchbacks! 'Cause they got to bend so much to get through the airways, that's why, the airways is so narrow!

MINER
Mice with hunchbacks, my arse! No bloody mouse would be seen dead in this hole. It's only us silly buggers who ever come down here.

MINER
Alright, alright, don't go frightening the lad. Don't worry Davy, they do this to all the new boys.

SARCASTIC MINER
He'll get used to it.

DAVY
Yes, I can get used to anything I suppose, but I don't have to like it, do I!

(A shot is fired. A loud bang makes Davy jump)
(Enter Mr Hughes, a foreman)

MR HUGHES
Where's that bloody Tom Dafis? I've been looking all over for him. And where's the Jones lad?

JOHN
Which one, there's half a dozen here!

MR HUGHES
Don't be clever! Oh, Hopkin! I might have guessed. The new lad, where is he?

DAVY
Here!

MR HUGHES
Answer next time and be quick about it! Right, you're working with Harry this morning on the haulage. You'll be keeping a hold on the pony while he checks the load. Then, when he gives the signal, let the horse walk on and you walk beside him. He won't need any encouragement. That old horse has been doing that job for seven years, so he knows exactly what to do, so don't be tempted to give him a whack if he stops. He won't move even if you do. He might have sensed some danger up ahead, like a loose rock in the roof or a broken rail don't ask me how he knows, he just does! Understand?

DAVY
Yes.

MR HUGHES
And you Hopkin, get back on the door, I'll speak to you later!

JOHN
But I haven't finished my butties yet!

MR HUGHES
Hard luck! You'll have to leave them for the mice, won't you, or stick the lot in your gob! *(Exit Mr Hughes)* It's big enough!

JOHN *(to Davy)*
You lucky bugger, working with the horses and with Soldier, he's my favourite! That spiteful old sod threw me off the job because Harry moaned about me to him. *(John exits)*

DAVY
This gas is dangerous stuff, isn't it.

MINER
Bloody right it is. It creeps up on you without you knowing it. Years ago they used canaries to warn you, kept in a cage they was and hung from the roof.

DAVY
Canaries! How?

MINER
Well as soon as the canary breathed in the gas they'd drop down dead. Boom! Like that!

DAVY
Poor old canaries.

MINER
What you talking about, poor old canaries, it's better than poor old pit men dropping down dead!

DAVY
Yes, I suppose so.

MINER
What do you mean, you suppose so? There's no bloody suppose about it. Hoi, Albert, what have you been teaching this lad of yours?

MR JONES *(Mr Jones enters)*
How are you doing, son?

DAVY
I'm okay. I've been working with the horses.

MR JONES
That's a good job, you're lucky.

DAVY
Hoi Dad, why does Mesach sit by himself, what's he reading?

MR JONES
The Bible of course, what else. His family have been big in the Chapel for years. Lot of good it's done him. *(Dismissively)*

DAVY
Don't let Mam hear you talking like that! *(Mr Jones looks at him and shakes his head in disbelief)*

MINER *(A miner enters)*
Joe's coming, get ready!

MINERS
La la la la,
Da da de da *(The Wedding March)*

MINER
Joe's a married man now, so you'd better behave yourselves. Very respectable.

MINER
No need for a hot water bottle now Joe, eh!

MINER
No more buttie jams for your snappin' now, it'll be bacon and chunks of pork.

MINER
To keep his strength up.

MINER
Aye.

MINER
Well he never needed it before, did he. He never did any work. I wouldn't get married for all the tea in China.

MINER
Who'd want to marry you!

JOE
When you are all finished I'll tell you something – what have you got to look forward to when you finish work tonight? Nothing, coz you're all single. You get home, have a bite to eat then off to bed. There's no one waiting for you. Your mam if you're lucky, but it's not the same as having a wife. When I get home my Margaret's ready at the door waiting with a smile and a cuddle. The water is boiling for my bath and half a pound of bacon ready for the pan as soon as I get out. *(Ring. Ring. Ring. Snappin' time finishes. The men move to their tasks quietly)*

SARCASTIC MINER
It won't last.

JOE
Maybe not but while it does I'm the happiest man in the world.

FOREMAN
What's this, a picnic! Where's Twm Davis?

MINER
Haven't seen him all shift.

94

FOREMAN
Well when you do *(emphasise)* see him tell him I want him down at No 4 *(Exit)*

MINER
Are you working at the weekend, Davy?

DAVY
No, we're all going to Rhyl for the day.

MINER
Very nice!

DAVY
Humph!

MINER
What's wrong with that!

DAVY
I'm going to be stuck with me Mam and my sister. She'll be moaning all day.

MINER
Who, your little sister?

DAVY
Ah, the both of them! Hoi, I've got to go now, Harry Horses will be waiting for me!

MR JONES
Heh, son, remember, use your brains not your back, you've got eight hours of this. You won't last till the end of the shift if you go at it like a bull at a gate.

LATER

John is opening the ventilation door.

JOHN
You loading those tubs a bit heavy, aren't you? The old horse can hardly pull them, he's nearly on his knees.

MINER
Shut up! When you've been down here twenty years, then you can talk. Until then, mind your own business! I got a wife and three kids to look after.

JOHN
The poor horse has done one shift already and now he's going out to do another, he should have a rest.

MINER
I told you to shut up! You're going to get a thump if you open your mouth again.

(*He holds a lamp close to John's face.*) EXIT.

DAVY
I wouldn't have dared say anything to Harry, he can be a nasty sod. You must really like the horses, John.

JOHN
Well aye, of course I do! I've told you before, I want to get a job with the horses one day, as a haulier. It's rotten the way they get treated by some of these old buggers. You can trust them horses better than some of the blokes down here. And they don't play tricks on you, neither. Anyway, I've got to mind these doors and you'd better shift as well or you'll have the bugger chasing you.

MINER (*Off stage*)
Hurry up, will you!

JOHN
What did I say?

(*Davy exits*) (*John returns to his stool by the door. The stage is in total darkness except for the glow given off by John's lamp which hangs on a nail above his head. The light slowly diminishes to total darkness.*) (*The sound of tubs clattering and muffled explosions can be heard in a distant part of the mine.*)

CURTAINS

SCENE 1

THE JONES'S BACK KITCHEN

(The table is piled high with all the requirements of a trip to the seaside. Straw hat, basket, thermos, parasol and a pile of beef paste sandwiches)

MR JONES
Uhm - putting powder on, are you? *(He puts his arm around her waist)*

MRS JONES
Well, yes, you know how chapped my face gets with all that salty air. Anyway, you want me to look nice, don't you? I need something to brighten myself up. Hey! Your jacket stinks of mothballs!

MR JONES
Well I haven't worn it since Jack's funeral. Anyway, the sea air will soon blow that away. *(Puts jacket over chair, puts kettle on the hob, exits back door)*

MRS JONES *(from the bottom of the stairs)*
Ruth! Davy! Hurry up you two, we're going to be late. *(Boiling kettle whistles. Mrs Jones makes a pot of tea) (enter Davy from the bottom of the stairs, goes to back door)* Take this up to Taid and mind you don't spill it! Ruth! *(From bottom of the stairs)* Ruth! What are you doing? Hurry up!

RUTH
I'm coming, Mama.

MRS JONES
At last! We're going to be late! *(The two children run down the stairs and out into the backyard to the back door as Mr Jones re-enters)*

MR JONES *(lifting the kettle)*
Where's my hot water?

MRS JONES
I used it for Taid's cup of tea. He'll never get out of bed if he doesn't have his cup of tea first.

MR JONES
I was going to have a shave with that! *(He refills the kettle)*

MRS JONES
I hope he'll be all right while we are away, he's not looking too good this morning. I've asked next door to look in while we are away to make sure he's all right.

MR JONES
Not on your life! You're not letting any of those buggers in here!

MRS JONES
Oh, calm down! I've only spoken to Mrs Hopkin, not him.

MR JONES
Well, I hope you've hidden the rent money! And empty that vase while you're at it. *(He points to the vase)*

RUTH *(enter Ruth, sobbing)*
Mama! Davy wouldn't let me use the lavatory and I'm wet now!

MRS JONES
Aww! Come on Shino, come upstairs and we'll change those wet knickers. *(Enter Davy)* You big bully, look what you've done to Ruth! We've saved up all year for this trip so don't start. Just make sure you wash behind your ears or I'll be starting. *(She goes upstairs with Ruth)* And your feet! You'll be walking around in your shorts, so I want you to look clean. I don't want people to think we're common. *(Exit upstairs)* *(Davy washes his feet in a bowl)*

MR JONES *(shouting up to Mrs Jones)*
Bring her bucket and spade, it's in the box under the bed. *(Speaking to Davy)* You've upset Mam already! *(Mr Jones examines a pile of sandwiches on the table and takes one)* Dew, there's enough beef paste sandwiches here to feed an army. *(Davy reaches for one)* Don't, Davy! Wait until your mother comes down. You know what she's like!

(Enter Mrs Jones and Ruth with bucket and spade) *(Ruth puts bucket and spade on the table)*

MRS JONES
Not on the tablecloth! It's clean on this morning. On the floor with it, mucky thing! *(Ruth puts it on the floor by her chair)* We'll have some of these sandwiches before we go.

DAVY
But they're all beef paste!

MRS JONES
Sorry, your lordship, not good enough for you? You'll be glad of these later on today! *(To Ruth)* Come on, Shino, let me do your hair before we go. Now sit still. Now listen, I don't want you wandering off on your own when we get to the seaside.

MR JONES
You might get kidnapped by a travelling showman!

RUTH
What's kidnapped, Mama?

MRS JONES
Oh! Go on you! Dad is being silly. *(She finishes combing Ruth's hair)* There you are, you look a picture. Now stay there until we are ready to go. I've got to go upstairs to see Taid, so be a good girl and don't move and don't go out into the yard. I don't want you getting dirty. *(Exits upstairs)* *(from the top of the stairs)* Get those things into the bags, it's getting late. I didn't realise the time, and put Ruth's hat on and her cardi and put her mac in the bag, you never know what the weather will do. And don't forget her bucket and spade either!

MR JONES *(Mr Jones nods his head impatiently)*
Come here, Shino, let's put your cardigan on and your hat. There you are, lovely! And put your raincoat in the bag.

RUTH
But it doesn't rain at the seaside, does it Dada?

MR JONES
It might. Hey, you're not going to Africa you know! It's only Rhyl we're going to!

RUTH
I want to take Topsy with me.

MR JONES
You can't.

RUTH
I want to!

MR JONES
There's not enough room! *(Getting angry)* We said last night she couldn't go. There's not enough room! *(Ruth starts to cry) (Mr Jones pulls it out of the cupboard along with crashing pots and pans)* All right! All right! Take Topsy, but if you lose her it will be your own fault. *(Mr Jones plonks Topsy in front of Ruth)*

RUTH
I want to take my kite too.

MR JONES
NO!

RUTH
Taid made it special for me so I could take it to the seaside. He said there's more wind there.

MR JONES
NO! *(Ruth sulks)(enter Mrs Jones)* How's Dad?

MRS JONES
He's very pale. Go upstairs and see for yourself. *(Exit Mr Jones upstairs)* Come on you two, we're going to be late for the bus and then we'll miss the train! *(Exit front door) (the bucket and spade are left behind) (Mr Jones takes a last look about the kitchen and exits. The front door slams shut. Lights start going down on the bucket and spade left behind. Seconds later the kitchen door opens, he charges in and pulls out the kite from behind the sideboard and exits)*

MRS JONES *(peering in through the kitchen door)*
Have we got everything?

MR JONES
Got everything! Of course we got everything. There's nothing left.

SCENE 2

PORTER
Chester! Chester! Change here for all stations to Holyhead. Chester! Change here for Birkenhead Woodside. *(The family spread out along the platform frantically looking for an empty compartment to call their own)*

MR JONES
Come on! There's room in here, sit there with your face to the sea. *(No sooner have they settled than a drunken passenger enters)*

DRUNK
Does this train stop at Clandudno? I hope so, I can't swim! Tee-hee!

RUTH
Where's the sea, Dada?

DAVY
It's all buildings, Dad!

MR JONES
Yes I know! *(Impatiently)* But wait till the train starts and you'll see it soon enough.

(The drunken man lurches towards the door)

DRUNK
Outa my way, I got to get a drink. Ooh! It's too late. *(The drunkard falls back into the corner seat to the sound of clanking bottles)*

DRUNK
Ooh! I had some here all the time, tee-hee! *(He searches for a bottle opener. He opens the bottle)* Have a sip! Go on! 'Ave one, go on!

MR JONES
No! No thank you.

DRUNK
Is that your Missus? *(He goes quiet for a few seconds. Suddenly he springs to life again)* Eh! Do you want a drink Missus? *(He waves the bottle at Mrs Jones)* No?! Eee! You don't know what you're missing. It's lovely, nectar, the drink of the gods. Tee-hee.

MRS JONES
You're drunk!

DRUNK
No I'm not! It's this train, it's jolting! Eee! It's lovely being drunk. There's nowt better. I could drink a gallon of the stuff. Don't you take a drink Mister? I don't blame you! You don't want to end up like me! Drunk. I'm telling you, nowt good comes of drinking. *(He goes to sleep. He wakes up again)*

DRUNK
Hello little girl, are you going on your holidays? Where are you going?

RUTH
Rhyl!

DRUNK
I'm going to Clan…Clan…Clandudno. I wanted to go to Bla…to Bla…to poo…poo… Blackpool! It's easi…it's easi… It's easier to say for one thing! And it's a lot closer. The wife's sisters got a boarding-house there in Clandudno, not Blackpool. *(He mutters to himself)*

RUTH
Why does he smell funny Dada?

MRS JONES
Shush!

TICKET COLLECTOR
Tickets please!

DRUNK *(the drunk automatically reaches for his pocket and then stops)*
Tickets again! How many times do you want to see them?

TICKET COLLECTOR
I haven't seen your ticket before, sir.

DRUNK
Well you're the only one who hasn't seen it. Everybody else from here to Manchester Victoria has!

TICKET COLLECTOR
I have to punch your ticket sir.

DRUNK
Punch my ticket! Who do you think you are? Joe Louis? There'll be more holes in this ticket than in a string bag.
(Ticket collector punches the ticket)

TICKET COLLECTOR
Tickets please. *(He inspects the tickets)* How old is the boy?

MRS JONES
Thirteen and three quarters.

TICKET COLLECTOR
Hmmm. *(He turns to leave the compartment)*

DRUNK
Down with authority, down with class distinction!

TICKET COLLECTOR
Is this gentleman causing you any distress, Madam?

MRS JONES
No, no…

(Exit ticket inspector)

DRUNK *(sarcastically)*
Is this gentleman causing you any distress, Madam?

DAVY
Eh, Dad, how come at home I'm fourteen but on the train I'm only thirteen?

MR JONES
Be quiet!

DRUNK
Punch me ticket! I'd like to punch him! I wish I could be drunk every day, but I can't afford it. I've spent all my money on beer and I've got none left now to buy any more. There's a state isn't it! Oh! I'm in a terrible state. I'm so ashamed of myself…Eh! It's lovely being drunk! You look as if you like a drink Mister, like to get drunk as well? I bet you do, don't you! Well, you've never lived then! There's nowt better than being drunk. Eee! It's lovely… It's a terrible comedown being drunk. You don't mind me smoking my pipe do you?

MRS JONES
Yes!

DRUNK
Well you better get out then!

MRS JONES
Come and sit on my knee, Ruth. *(She beckons to Ruth)*

PORTER
Holywell Junction! Holywell Junction!

PASSENGER *(A new passenger appears at the door)*
Any room for a little 'un?

MR JONES
Ugh! Where have I heard that before, I think half of Lancashire must be heading to the seaside today. *(Everybody squeezes up)*

102

RUTH
Seagulls!

MR JONES
That's a sure sign we're nearly there! *(The kite slips off the luggage rack but it is suspended in mid-air by its guy rope. Davy pushes it back onto the luggage rack, turns and sees the lighthouse.)*

DAVY
The lighthouse! Hurrah! Hurrah! It's Rhyl! We're here!

MR JONES *(He points to the lighthouse)*
We'll go for a walk up there if we've got time. Check that we haven't left anything! *(Exit family, the drunk drops an empty whisky bottle into Mrs Jones's bag and falls asleep.)*

PORTER *(Enter left)*
Rhyl! Rhyl! All stations to Llandudno! *(Exit right)*

DRUNK *(Drunk awakes with a start)*
Clandudno? Clandudno! Hey! That's my stop! *(He staggers out of the compartment and onto the platform) (Exit left)*

MR JONES
Just check and make sure we haven't left anything. *(He gets down on his hands and knees and pulls out Topsy)* Look! After all the fuss you made about bringing Topsy, too! *(Ruth grabs hold of Topsy)*

MRS JONES
Oh! No! It's raining! *(Exit station with umbrella)*

SCENE 3

(The Jones's enter onto the promenade. A brass band is playing in the distance. The sound of children laughing and seagulls mewing. All the seats are full except for one with an old man/couple/an exceptionally large person sitting in the middle of it)

MR JONES
He (*she*) might move over and give us some room. (*They look at the occupant expectantly but there is no movement. They sit either side of the occupant. Mr Jones enters with a deckchair and deliberately makes a mess of setting it up. The children laugh and tell him how to do it properly. Mrs Jones knows that it is a joke and sighs patronisingly.*)

MRS JONES
You do the same thing every year! (*The occupant looks on with disgust and rises to leave. All the Jones's take over the seat*)

RUTH
Donkeys! Look! Can I have a ride on the donkeys?

MRS JONES
Wait a minute, we've only just got here.

RUTH
I want to ride on the donkeys!

MR JONES
Go and make a sandcastle!

RUTH
I want a donkey!

MR JONES
No! You are too heavy!

RUTH
Jesus had a ride on a donkey. Miss Jenkins at Sunday school said so.

MRS JONES
Oh! In a minute. Just wait till we've sorted things out.

RUTH
Where's my bucket, Mama?

MRS JONES
You left it at home and after me telling you to look after it!

RUTH
But I want it!

MRS JONES
Well, you can't have it. It's in the house where you left it!

RUTH
But I want it! (*Ruth starts to cry*)

MRS JONES
Oh! For goodness sake, it's your fault and I'm not buying you another one.

MR JONES
Oh! They are only threepence.

MRS JONES
No! That's threepence wasted. She's got one at home.

MR JONES
We've come all this way and she's got nothing to play with. It's only a bucket, it's only threepence.

MRS JONES
We're not spending thruppence on a bucket. Go and look for some shells, Shino and bring them back here and we'll sort them out.

MR JONES
What is she going to put them in when she finds them? She hasn't got a bucket!

MRS JONES
Why does she have to have a bucket? She can put them in a tin or something. (*She rummages in her bag for a tin*)

MR JONES
A tin?! What tin? Eh! Don't take those sandwiches out of the tin. They'll be covered in sand in no time.

DAVY
Dad, you could buy a tin of toffees from the kiosk over there and…

MR JONES
A tin of toffees! What good would that do?

DAVY
Well you can empty them out and Ruth can use the tin to put some shells in.

MR JONES
That'll work out more expensive than buying her a new bucket! Ok, I've got an idea. Here is a tanner, get Mam's favourites – humbugs in a tin like you said, not a bag.
(*Exit Davy slowly*) Hurry up! Or you'll be all day! (*Exit Davy*)

(*Mr Jones looks through his binoculars and sees some bathing beauties in the distance. He smiles. A passerby asks what he can see.*)

PASSERBY
What can you see?

MR JONES
Just a wave splashed up against that old lady! The tide must be coming in!

PASSERBY
Yes. I bet. (*Smirks*)

MRS JONES (*Enter Mrs Jones*)
See anything interesting?

MR JONES (*He quickly redirects the binoculars*)
Not much. (*He sits down*) (*enter Davy with a tin of humbugs*)

MRS JONES (*she opens the tin and empties out the humbugs*) Now, let's see Davy's bright idea. There it is, a bucket, (She holds the empty tin aloft) for your shells! Come on Ruth and Davy, let's look for some shells on the beach and we might find some treasure!

MR JONES
Keep some for me! (*He falls asleep. Lights down.*)
(*Lights up. Enter Ruth and Davy. Ruth hits the deck chair with her stick and startles Mr Jones*)
MR JONES
Ahh! Find any treasure?

RUTH
Coral! (*She holds a red shell*)

MR JONES
Nah! Coral is from hot places like Africa and India! Not from here, the Irish Sea! (*He points*) It's too cold for them here, they'd turn blue! (*To David*) What's that you got?

DAVY
It's a cup. I won it on the hoopla stall.

MR JONES
Where's the saucer?

DAVY
I didn't get one of those. The hoop wouldn't fit over it.

MR JONES
No saucer! What's the good of that?! We'll have to come back next year to win one! (*He reads the inscription along the side*) A present from Rhyl. Pity you didn't win an egg cup! It would have matched the one we've got from New Brighton!

MR JONES
What's that you got?

(*Mrs Jones tends to Ruth*)

DAVY
The Chronicle. (*He reads the headline*) Harry Huxley, The Chronicle's Man of Mystery.

MR JONES
Who?

DAVY
Harry Huxley! Will be joining in the fun at Rhyl today. If you spot him and you got a copy of the Chronicle you could win ten shillings. He'll be walking along the prom between the Funfair and the Winter Gardens. Watch out for the cactus, missus!

MR JONES
Well I'm not traipsing around this place on the off chance I'll bump into Harry Huxley. Give it here.

DAVY
Aw Dad, I wanted that.

MR JONES
Can't let Mam see it. You know what she's like. (*He hides the Chronicle*)
Here's tuppence... And take Ruth with you... And don't lose sight of her... And keep hold of her hand. (*Exit Davy and Ruth*) (*He settles back in a deckchair, time passes*) (*he stares through the binoculars into the far distance*)

(*Davy enters*)

MR JONES
Where's Ruth?

DAVY
I dunno.

MR JONES
There's a hat just like hers bobbing up and down over there! (*He points seawards*) I told you not to let go of her!

DAVY
She was here a minute ago!

MRS JONES
Ruth! Oh! Where could she have got to? You were told not to lose sight of her! (*Exit left or right*)

MR JONES (*enter Ruth and a married couple*)
Where have you been? We've been looking all over for you! (*Ruth is licking an ice cream*) I hope she hasn't caused you any trouble.

COUPLE
No, of course not! She's been as good as gold haven't you? (*Ruth nods her head*) (*everybody exchanges pleasantries*) (*the married couple exits*)

MRS JONES
Where have you been? I told you not to go with strangers!

MR JONES
They don't look like kidnappers to me!

DAVY
Can I have that sixpence, Dad?

MR JONES
What for? Do you think I'm made of money.

DAVY
You gave sixpence to Ruth.

MR JONES
What for, I said!

DAVY
To go to the shops.

MR JONES
What shops?

DAVY
Down there. (*Davy points*)

MR JONES
What shops is down there? (*He looks in that direction*)

DAVY
Well… I don't know… There's a Lady in a Goldfish Bowl. And a Woman with a Beard.

MR JONES
They're those freakshow places, you don't want to throw money away on those places.

MRS JONES (indignantly)
Indeed not! What would the neighbours think, a woman with a beard.

MR JONES
The neighbours! The neighbours! What chance is there of any of the neighbours being here today and seeing us!

MRS JONES
That's not the point... How can people do things like that, showing themselves up.

MR JONES
Well what else can they do, it's the only way they can make a living. What's the time?

MRS JONES
Half past four! It's getting late. We should be getting up to the fair! (*They pack up their stuff*) (*Lights down*)

(*Later*) (*lights up*)

MR JONES
Come on, hurry up! I don't think anyone from the Mothers' Union has seen us yet (*exit family from the Woman with a Beard booth*)

(*lights down*)

SCENE 4

(The fairground at Rhyl.) (A banner displays CAPTAIN CARRUTHERS' BULLDOG BOXERS. Enter the family along the front of the stage apron. Tabs closed. From behind the tabs steps a smartly dressed military type, Captain Carruthers, as painted on the hoarding, and manager of the boxing booth, together with one or two weak -looking characters in boxing shorts who start sparring in a very ineffectual manner. The drunk appears and the family avoid contact but to no avail.)

DRUNK
Hey up! Fancy meeting you here, small world isn't it!

CAPTAIN
Come on, come on, step up! Any of you brave lads willing to take on my boys? One guinea for any man who can go three rounds with any of my boys. What about you sir? Fancy your chances, if you think you are man enough to don the gloves and partake of the noble art and last three rounds with one of my boys. The bouts will be arranged strictly according to the Queensbury rules, three three-minute rounds and a minute's breather at the end of each round and if you're still standing at the end of three rounds it's a lovely guinea for you!

BYSTANDER
And a silver cup paid for by public subscription!

BYSTANDER
And a stretcher!

CAPTAIN
Come on gentlemen, make your minds up. We've already got some game fellows in the booth, we are ready to start the show, a guinea for a winner! Just for three rounds!

MR JONES
I went three rounds with Johnny Bashem. *(Absentmindedly, trancelike, he stares into the distance)*

MRS JONES
That was fifteen years ago!

MR JONES
Eh? What? *(He wakes up from his trance and turns to Mrs Jones)*

MRS JONES
That was fifteen years ago, these lot are half your age.

MR JONES
Hoi, I'll have a go at that!

MRS JONES
Oh no! You'll get hurt!

MR JONES
I used to box every week down at the club. *(insistently)*

MRS JONES
That was years ago, I'm telling you, you'll get hurt.

MR JONES
Don't be daft, against them? They couldn't knock the skin off a rice pudding. Anyway it's worth the risk for two guineas, that's three days wages, I could buy you that a new coat you're always on about, I'm going to take a chance. 'Ere you are, I'll have a go!

BYSTANDER
Hey lad, thee dost not want to go up wi' them. They's vicious buggers, they'd fight for a crust of bread. Aye, for nowt even.

BARKER
Ah, don't pay no attention to him, these fellows are all 'as beens. They been flat on their backs so many times old Carruthers uses the soles of their boots to advertise the next show, give the old one-two *(he spars)* and they are goners, dead as a door nail, well not dead, but you know what I mean!

CAPTAIN
Well come on then, we haven't got all day. *(Mr Jones is pulled onto the stage. The Barker disappears off stage)* what's your name, get his coat off. *(To assistant)* We've got enough now, we'll start.

MR JONES
Jones.

CAPTAIN
Eh?

MR JONES
Jones, Albert Jones. *(Cheers and groans coming from inside the tent)*

CAPTAIN
Where you from?

MR JONES
Wrexham.

CAPTAIN
You Welsh?

MR JONES
Yes.

CAPTAIN
Well done sir, well done, come forward, come forward, I can see the spirit of Owen Glendower lives on, Mr Lloyd George would be proud of you. Take your shirt off son. *(To an assistant)* Hurry up with those gloves!

Ladies and gentlemen, welcome! This afternoon, Captain Carruthers, myself, *(he takes a bow)* Captain Carruthers' boxing booth is proud to present some of the finest amateur boxers ever to grace the ring and as an opener we have a challenger, Arthur –

MR JONES
Albert!

CAPTAIN
Arthur Jones, against one of our new recruits, battling Billy Herbert from Wolverhampton. Show your appreciation and give a big hand for the challenger, Arthur Jones!

BYSTANDER
Battling Billy, he's crafty he is, he is left-handed so he can catch you out, people don't expect a left-hander.

BYSTANDER
Hoi! Give him one for me will you, he flattened my brother a few weeks ago… After the bell!

MR JONES *(angrily but ignored nevertheless)*
Albert!

(The crowd cheers and the tent flap opens whilst a bruised challenger stumbles out from the inside, held up by his wife)

BYSTANDER
A big hand for the brave challenger my foot! *(Sarcastically)* A big hand for the loser more like!

CAPTAIN
Don't hit him too hard son, he might look tough but he's got a weak heart. *(The tabs open to reveal a tough -looking boxer surrounded by 'Seconds')*

CURTAINS CLOSE

SCENE 5

(In a railway carriage on the return journey, Albert turns to face the audience sporting a black eye and a red nose)

MRS JONES
We'll be able to see you coming down the road with that. I suppose her across the street will have something to say about it.

MR JONES
Very funny. Well it was worth it. Two guineas. Lucky though, I just swung out and caught him right on the nose. Slowed him down a bit, anyway, I didn't have to knock him out, just had to last three rounds.

MRS JONES
Do you want a beef paste sandwich?

MR JONES
If I have another of those sandwiches I'll be growing horns.
(Mrs Jones pours a cup of tea from a Thermos, he takes a sip and grimaces) What do they put in this tea, it tastes as if it's been stewed for a week! All right, you can tell me what she said now.

MRS JONES
What who said?

MR JONES
Who! Her with the turban of course, Gypsy Rose what's her name on the pier, waste of money if you ask me.

MRS JONES
Well why do you want to know then, if it's a waste of money? *(Emphasis)*

MR JONES
Oh come on, let me into your little secret.

MRS JONES
She said I should do something with figures.

MR JONES
So what does that mean? Get an office job… or do the Pools!

1st Man *(On the platform, two railway employees meet)*
How long are you going to keep us here, we've been running late all the way from Bangor.

2nd Man
Look it's no use complaining to me, control is sending a Special through, probably Territorials from the camp at Kinmel Bay, you'll just have to wait!

1st Man

Late again! How long this time! Well! *(Porter exits with a playful gesture as Ruth watches through the compartment window)*

RUTH

We're going to be two hours late, Mama.

MRS JONES

Two hours late! Oh yes and how do you know we're going to be two hours late?

RUTH

'Cos that man asked how late we were going to be and the other man went like this *(she lifts up two fingers)(Mr and Mrs Jones look at each other, perplexed)* Dada, why can't we always go to the seaside? I like playing on the sand.

DAVY

Yes, Dad. I want to come here next summer. Every summer, now I got a job and some money. It's the best place on earth. *(He falls back onto the seat playfully.)*

MR JONES

How do you know it's the best place on earth? You haven't been anywhere yet.

RUTH

Can we come back next week?

MR JONES

Wait, wait, I have to go to work!

RUTH

Why do you have to do? They can't make you.

MR JONES

No, but they can sack me, and then where would I get the pennies from to pay for the train? These are hard times for people like us, colliers like me and Uncle Arthur.

RUTH

What is hard times meaning, Dada?

MR JONES

Hard times? Low wages, never enough money to buy all the things we need, but I've always got enough pennies to buy dolly mixtures for my little Shino. Here. *(He reaches into his pocket and brings out a bag of sweets)(He leans back against the seat and rubs his head)* Ooh my head. I feel as if I've gone ten rounds with Joe Louis.

MRS JONES

Serves you right. You could have ended up in hospital!

MR JONES

Never mind, I got two quid, it was worth it. We'll all have fish and chips tonight. And *(emphasise)* a bottle of Vimto for you *(to Ruth) (Everybody cheers)*

114

Special train roars through, whistle blowing. Signal clatters. Toot toot! Wrexham train departs.

LIGHTS DOWN

CLOSE CURTAINS

SCENE 6

(The front door bangs open. The kitchen door opens. The family troop in and dump their things on the floor. They put their fish and chips and a bottle of Vimto on the table ready to be unwrapped)

MRS JONES
Put that kettle on, I'm absolutely parched. *(She kicks off her shoes)*

MR JONES
You should have got one at the station buffet.

MRS JONES
There wasn't enough time, we nearly missed the bus as it was, anyway I'm not paying tuppence for a cup of tea when we've got plenty here. And I could see Mr and Mrs Davies in there, they must have been shopping, she had a bag on the table, looked like she bought a hat, she'll be wearing that in chapel tomorrow, lah-di-dah. Humph!

MR JONES
Where's Dad? *(He puts the kettle on the gas ring.)*

MRS JONES
I'll go up to his room. *(Exit upstairs)* *(Meanwhile the children squabble. Ruth runs around with her kite)*

MR JONES
Help your mother and get the butties ready. *(He opens the back door and shouts)* Dad! Dad! *(To Ruth)* put that thing away! *(Ruth ignores him and carries on running)* Davy, get the plates out!

MRS JONES *(she enters from the bottom of the stairs)*
It's Taid. He's…he's…dead!

Mr Jones catches hold of Ruth.

LIGHTS DOWN
CURTAIN

A FEW DAYS LATER

MINER
Come on, Davy, break time. *(The miners trudge to the junction)*

MINER
How did it go last weekend?

DAVY
Eh?

MINER
Rhyl! Your trip to sunny Rhyl!

DAVY
Oh, Dad got a black eye, my sister Ruth got lost and Mam lost her temper as usual.

MINER
Never mind, it's payday today!

JOHN
Check your payslip carefully, Davy. The Management are always trying to find ways to cut the wages.

DAVY
But that would be dishonest, John, they wouldn't do us down would they? We're all working together, aren't we?

JOHN
Ha! The only time they get off their arses to do any work is when they're scheming to cut our rates. All them pay clerks is mammy's boys. They'd shit themselves if they was to come down here. And that chief cashier! He's the one what's encouraging them to cut our wages. Gives 'em a pat on the head if they can diddle us out of a shilling. What do they know, they couldn't dig enough coal to fill a pisspot.

1st MINER *(A miner leans over and whispers in Davy's ear)*
He's right, Davy bach. We've had to fight for everything we got, and we haven't got much. You'll find out soon enough, Davy.

JOHN
And don't be fooled by the size of the packet. It's a lot bigger than anything you'll ever get inside it! *(He moves away)*

2nd MINER
You don't want to pay no attention to that John Hopkin, he's a bit of a troublemaker, a bloody Commie if you ask me, like his father. But I'll say this for him, he's a better worker than that lazy old bugger.

JOHN *(Angrily)*
What if I am a Commie? If it was left to you lot we'd still be on £2 a week, you lot are too fond of touching your caps. *(He walks off singing)* Keep your hands upon your wages and your eyes upon the scales…

TWM DAVIS *(referring to the foreman)*
Have you seen him?

MINER
He's just been looking for you. You'll cop it one of these days. You can't hide from him forever. He's gone along No. 3 shaft.

TWM DAVIS
Oh bugger. *(Twm hurries after him)*

MINER
We ought to call him 'The Artful Dodger', ha ha!

(The miners settle down to enjoy their break)

MINER
Well, you been here a few weeks now, what do you think of pit work, Davy?

DAVY
Ugh, it's hard, hard, but everybody's been very helpful even though they've got their own work to do. I've got to know everybody very well.

MINER
Aye, we all get to know everybody very well in this place.

DAVY
Even Jack.

MINER
Ah, he's a good sort really, a bit short tempered that's all. Well he's been down here thirty years, and he's no better off than when he started. He's like the rest of us really. Pit work's no good, Davy. I've been in mines of one sort or another all my life, but when I was your age I was working the slate up near Corwen, there you got fresh air and the sky above your head, here you got a mile of rock. I've heard you are a clever lad, got a bit of a brain. You want to use it and get out of here. Soon as you can.

DAVY
Not much chance of that. I said I wanted to come here and me dad wants me here as well, we need the money.

MINER
Ah, don't we all. Heh! Remember to check your butties before you start eating, them cockroaches get everywhere.

DAVY
Ugh! There's a cockroach!

MINER
Well I warned you.

SARCASTIC MINER
Never mind, he'll get used to it.

JOHN
Keep your hands upon your wages and your eyes upon the scales. *(Sings to the tune of the last chords of Calon Lân)*

(The sound of stones falling from the roof. A miner looks up at the roof to check the extent of 'fritting'.)

MINER
That's fritting, that is *(to Davy)* but it's not serious, but when it really sets off *(emphasise)* start making your way to safety, get out of the way, quick, like when they start playing God save the King in the pictures. Ha ha.

DAVY
Why?

MINER
Because it might mean there's going to be a roof fall or a bloody big stone falling down. You don't want to be under that, do you!

MR HUGHES *(enter foreman/charge hand)*
Have you seen that bloody Twm Davis?

MINER
He's not here.

MR HUGHES *(angrier)*
Have you finished clearing that blockage in No. 3 shaft?

MINER
Give us a chance, will you, it only fell a quarter of an hour ago! Rome wasn't built in a day, you know!

MR HUGHES
I know but they did make a start! You'd better shift yourselves quick or it will be coming out of your wages.
(Some miners move towards the blockage)
(Exit foreman) And when you see that bloody Twm Davis tell him I'm up at No. 3 shaft!

MR JONES *(enter Mr Jones)*
Hello, son. *(Enter Twm Davis)*

MINER *(Miner peers through the gloom and the coal dust)*
I can see who is king in your house, you just been crowned. Ha ha.
(Mr Jones storms off in a bad mood) Tut tut. No sense of humour, no wonder, married to her!

TWM *(Twm Davis returns) (He checks his payslip)*
What! They've deducted a tanner, look at that! Read that! *(He waves his payslip)*

MINER *(He reads the payslip)*
All this was explained in the meeting on Thursday, why didn't you say something then, was you sleeping?

TWM
It's the bloody government, it's their doing.

MINER
It's the owners.

TWM *(indignantly)*
They're all the same.

JOHN
See what I told you Davy, check your payslip.
(The sound of fritting)

TWM
I'm sick of this bloody district, I want a transfer.

MINER
If you want a better job go to that bloody club of his and buy him a few whiskies. *(He points his thumb in the direction of the foreman's exit)*

TWM *(mumbling)*
I'll never do that!
(The sound of fritting)

(A miner leans over and takes a piece of food from the miner in front unawares. The miner looks the other way whilst chatting, the other miner takes a piece of food from the other side. He is spotted.)

MINER
Bugger off, will you! *(Laughing)*

DAVY
What did you used to do before you started here, Mr Hughes?

MINER
I was a pox doctor's clerk. *(Impatient)*

DAVY
A what!

MINER
School like yourself, twenty years ago. (Impatient)

MINER
Hey lads, here comes old Danny now, let's give it to him, loud and clear! How do Danny, we got a little song for you, come on then you lot:

What horse you got for us tonight Danny Jones?
What horse you got for us tonight Dan Jones?
Give us one who's handy
Don't give us one who's bandy
What horse you got for us Danny Jones!

DANNY
You daft beggars, get off to work before I put this brush to your backsides.

MINER
Very respectable, old Dan, never uses strong language. *(He looks at his watch and taps it)* Come on, duty calls!

(All the miners stand up wearily and exit to their work places)

A FEW MINUTES LATER

(A large section of roof falls down amid lots of noise and dust. Enter Davy and other miners in the state of shock and sit down to recover.)

BLACKOUT

MINER
Jesus Christ, that was close.

(A miner looks back to into the swirling dust and investigates the seriousness of the fall)

MINER
Bloody hell. Fifteen ton must've come down. It's lucky those steel arches held or we would all have gone west.

MINER
If that hole was any bigger we would have Kenrick's cows dropping down on us!

FOREMAN *(feigning ignorance)*
What's happened, anybody hurt?

MINER
No, thank Christ. The roof's dropped about fifteen ton.

FOREMAN
How long will it take to clear it? *(Feigning ignorance)*

MINER
About four hours.

FOREMAN
Four hours! I'll give you three. *(He makes a note in his record book)* Well, you had better get started then, hadn't you.

MINER
Alright, alright!
(The miners start to return to the area of the fall. Davy does not move)

DAVY
There's no lights, the fall has brought the cable down, we'll have to wait for an electrician.

FOREMAN
Come on, come on, get back to work. You got lamps, haven't you? Hey, you, get moving we've got a pile of rock to clear up. You're not on a bloody picnic!

DAVY *(Davy does not move)*
Bugger off! I could have been killed in there!

FOREMAN
Don't talk to me like that, you cheeky young sod.

DAVY
It was your job to check the roof was safe.

FOREMAN
The roof was safe! I looked at it! Now get on with clearing it, or do you want to end up in the manager's office? *(To the other miners)* Now lads, let's be having you or we'll get no coal out today. *(Exit right)*

DAVY
He looked at it! Well that makes it all right then, doesn't it! Useless bastard! *(Exit left)*

(The foreman/manager and a miner meet)

MINER (hesitantly)
Some of the men have been complaining about gas.

FOREMAN
What men? Who? C'mon, who?

MINER
Well, some of the afternoon shift.

FOREMAN
Who?

MINER
Well, I can't say, can I.

FOREMAN
Why not?

MINER
Well I can't, you know I can't.

FOREMAN
All right, all right! I'll test for the gas here, you go along to the turning and see if they've cleared that blockage. *(Exit right. When the miner disappears, he looks about him, he looks up, but does not test for gas. Exit left.)*

THE JONES'S BACK KITCHEN
A FEW WEEKS LATER

MRS JONES
(She enters from the staircase holding Mr Jones's overcoat) This coat needs airing, you haven't worn it since Dad's funeral last month. *(She brushes it and pulls a piece of paper out of a pocket and reads it, returns it and hangs it on a hook)*

MR JONES
There's some good stuff on in town this week. *(Reading the Wrexham Leader)* Bertram Mills Circus is in town. They've never been here before! They got some 'Cricketing Elephants!'

MRS JONES
What!

MR JONES
Jeanette's Cricketing Elephants it says here. See, they got cricket pads on their legs. *(He shows the advert)*

MRS JONES
Whatever next! How much to get in?

MR JONES
1/3 and 2/6

MRS JONES
How much! It's only ninepence in the pictures. Have a look what's on. No! We haven't got the money to be going to the pictures… Are they "talkies"?

MR JONES
Of course they're talkies, they're all talkies now!

MRS JONES
Oh, I'll never get used to sitting there dumb, you can't say a word now without someone shushing you! I liked the old silent films, you can't even whisper now without someone shhhhhh!

MR JONES *(exasperated)*
Look, do you want to go or not!

MRS JONES
Yes, all right, but only in the ninepennies.

MR JONES
Well listen woman! Starting next week in the Hippodrome it's "Fashions of 1934" with Bette Davis and Dick Powell with 200 streamlined beauties. You'll have to wear a disguise, don't want the Mother's Union seeing you there!

MRS JONES
You can forget that one!

MR JONES
Ugh! "Four Frightened People", the Glynn; "Lazy River", the Empire; "Flying Down to Rio", Majestic. It's a musical, Fred Aster (sic), Ginger Rogers… you'll like that. Well that's something nice to look forward to. We'll go and see that. Oh! What am I talking about? I'm on nights all next week. Well we could go on Saturday night I suppose, yes, I haven't been to town on a Saturday night for ages, and I can wear my swanky overcoat. No use keeping it just for funerals! *(Mrs Jones goes to hang the coat)* Hoi, let me try it on. *(She hands him the coat. He admires himself in the mirror. He puts on a slouch hat)* James Cagney!

MRS JONES
Humph!

LIGHTS DOWN. MUSIC. THE CARIOCA FROM "FLYING DOWN TO RIO"

UNDERGROUND
A few days later.

JOHN

You're early aren't you, you still got a few minutes before the end of the shift, don't let the Overman catch you, he'll be putting your name down in his book.

DAVY

He won't, he's down at the far end. Keep your eyes open for him just in case or the both of us will end up in his book!

JOHN

I'm all right, I'm staying on tonight.

DAVY

Bloody hell, you're doing another turn, you must be keen.

JOHN

Well aye! I need the money. The Town's playing Tranmere Rovers tomorrow, I don't want to miss that!

DAVY

You're working here all night just so you can afford to go and see a game of football tomorrow… Tch, I could understand it if they was any good…

JOHN

Whaddaya mean any good, they are good, they haven't lost a game and Tranmere's top of the division! I'm not going to miss that, the ground's going to be packed, half the town will be there! The town will be going up this season!

DAVY

Well they'll be going without me, I can't afford to see a game of football!

JOHN

No wonder you can't afford it, you give all your money to your mam.

DAVY

Give it? She takes it. Nah, I just can't afford it.

MINER

No, and Wrexham can't afford to buy any decent players neither! This new centre forward they got from Sunderland isn't up to much so I heard.

JOHN

Well give him a chance, you want to knock him down before he's had a chance to prove himself.

MINER

They'll never get anywhere without decent players, they just haven't got the money. They lost over a thousand pound last season.

MINER
A thousand pound! And all out of the Directors' own pockets too!

JOHN
Our pockets you mean!

MINER
You've started him off again.

MINER *(Mumbles)*
They got more money than sense, those buggers.

JOHN
Eh, this is a funny thing, the last time Wrexham played Tranmere it was abandoned because of fog. Boxing Day, it was. I was with me dad and you know what the ref's name is for tomorrow's match?

MINER
No.

JOHN
Fogg! Funny, innit?

(Miner enters from the coal face. He joins the others and takes a swig from his water bottle) (it is empty)

MINER
It's as hot as hell up there man, not enough air there for human life.

MINER
You'll be all right then, Tommy!

MINER
Ha, ha, very funny. It's no bloody joke, it's wrong up there, I told the boss but you know what his attitude is, 'If you don't like it, pack up and go home!' Go home! Ugh! With no wages, no job, the missus moaning, the kids screiching! I'm glad I'm not working up there tonight. I'm thinking of asking for a transfer!

(Three short explosions emanate from the coalface)

JOHN
Well if you want a better job you should buy him a few whiskies at that club he goes to! *(He points his thumb towards the coalface)* Hoi, shut up, he's coming.

OVERMAN FIRER
I've just brought ten ton down, that will keep you going for an hour or two so there's plenty to be getting on with.

MINER
Is it safe for gas?

OVERMAN FIRER
Of course it is! I wouldn't have fired the shots if there was gas, would I?

MINERS *(grumbling from the men)*
Mmm, Agh.

OVERMAN FIRER
Look, if it's safe for me, it's safe for you.

OVERMAN FIREMAN
Are you doing a double turn tonight?

MINER
No thanks, I want to get home to my bed, I'm buggered.

OVERMAN FIREMAN
Ah… you young lads, you don't know what work is! What about you? *(The noise of tubs quietens as men finish their shift)*

JOHN
Yes, I'll stop on.

OVERMAN FIRER
That's the spirit, there's plenty of work for you. We won't be bothering about repairing; we got a lot of tubs to get out so you can stay on the air doors. I'll see you later.

JACKIE
(A bell rings in a distant shaft.) There's the bell, that's me finished for tonight, I'm off. See you tomorrow after the game.

OVERMAN FIRER
Is that Jackie? Hoi, Jackie! Where are you off to? You said you was going to do a double tonight.

JACKIE
Nah, I changed me mind, I don't feel well, I'm off home.

OVERMAN FIRER
Now you tell me! Where am I going to get an engineman at this time of night? Oh, go on then. *(He shouts to the miners)* Come on you lot, get back to your places, we've got a lot of stuff to move tonight! *(Miner's exit to their places of work. Lights down. Quiet. Noise of tubs recommences as the shift resumes work)*

LATER. PAST MIDNIGHT. EARLY HOURS OF THE MORNING.

Set for coal mine includes ladders and trapdoors to represent different levels and inclines. It is break time. The miners are crouched together, chatting. A distant loud noise is heard.

MINER *(Bang bang)*
What the hell…

MINER
Christ that was big!

MINER
Sounded like a pressure hose.

MINER
It was bigger than that!

MINER
Far end of 29 cutting, wasn't it, let's go down and see what happened.
(Incredibly loud bangs, dust, falling rocks and flames)

MINER
Stay where you are and keep calm.

MINER *(Miner runs past)*
Get out, get out, quick as you can!

MINER
What's happened?

MINER
The whole of 29 is going up! Get out! Get out!

(A miner enters, running, stumbling, and absolutely black.)

ALBERT
Hold on, hold on! Where are you going?

(He falls into the arms of Albert)

MINER
Who is it?

ALBERT
Jesus Christ, it's Ron Evans! *(He turns away and mumbles)* What a mess.
Hey, Ron old lad, what have you been doing!

RON
Albert, is it you?

ALBERT
Yes, of course it is.

RON
It is you, isn't it?

ALBERT
Yes, it's Albert, it's Albert.

RON
I'm glad you're safe, I thought you got knocked down in the blast.

ALBERT
Hey, I'm glad you're safe too, boy!

RON
Help me Albert, help me will you.

ALBERT
Of course, old pal.

RON
Don't let the roof come down on me, will you? Don't let the roof come down on me. I was always a good friend to you wasn't I, Albert? Don't let the roof come down on me. *(long silence)*

MINER
Put this under his head *(he takes off his shirt)* I said this would happen one day, too much gas, no checks.

ALBERT
He won't need that, he's gone.

MINER
He's dead, Christ he's dead! I said it would happen one day.

ALBERT
He was a good bloke, he was a good man. *(He turns away shocked)*

MINER
I said it would…

MINER
Never mind that now, how the bloody hell we going to get out of here? The roads will be blocked to the cage.

ALBERT
You don't know that for sure! We'll get out, I know a way!
(John runs past)

ALBERT
John, where you going?

JOHN
Me dad's down there, I got to help him, who's coming with me?

ALBERT
Don't be daft lad, you can't go down there, it's not possible. Everything's burning, props, dust, brattice, everything. It's hell! That's all you can call it, hell!

JOHN
Please, please help me, me dad's down there!

ALBERT
It's no use I tell you, there's no way along there, it's not possible! There's falls everywhere, the whole place is on fire! You'll never get through.

MINER
It's like a volcano. There was lumps of coal jumping out at me, spitting at me they was.

ALBERT
Stay with us, John, we'll get you out.

MINER
I know your dad's down there but… Well… Maybe he got out another way.

JOHN
Me dad's down there I tell you. Will somebody come with me?

MINER
You can't go down there, the whole road's gone, all the props is knocked out and the roof's dropped.

JOHN *(a miner emerges from the glowing shaft)*
Have you seen me dad, Jim Hopkin, you was working with him on number 14 face wasn't you, you must have seen him, why didn't you bring him out with you? Will somebody come with me… Well bugger the lot of you, I'm going back to look for me dad!

MINER *(A miner grapples with John)*
Don't go, John, there's a wall of fire and God knows how far back that goes.

JOHN
To hell with you!
(Exit into the shaft)

MINER
John, Johnny! That's the last we'll see of him!

MINER
Ah! Shut up!

MINER
What about us, how the bloody hell are we going to get out of here, I got a wife and kids.

MINER
So have I, we all have!

MINER
Please Lord if you bring me out safe I won't ask for anything ever again! Our Father who art in heaven... *(He is smacked)*

MINER
Stupid bastard! *(Under his breath)* That's not going to get us out, stupid bastard!

MINER
Well I'm staying, we'll be safe under those rails. *(He moves under the roof supports) (crash. The roof falls on the miner. The other miners clear away the fallen rubble)*

MINER
Watch out! *(The roof falls)*

MINER
We're going to die, we're going to die, our Father who art in heaven...

MINER
Get some props, we got a man buried here.

MINER
Joe help us for Christ's sake help us, what are you standing around for, help us get him out for Christ's sake! We can get to him. Drag him out, pull him by his arms!

MINER
He's too heavy, it's these bloody rocks. Shift them!

MINER
No, no, there's ten ton of rock on him. Listen, listen, he's dead. We can't do anything for him, he's gone and we've got to save ourselves.

MINER
I know. I know how we can get out of here. Just off 142 Deep there's this passage. The airway leads to the main road from there. It was blocked off years ago but we can break through it. I know that section, I worked it for two years. *(He grabs a pick)*

MINER
Well what are we standing around waiting for, let's get going.

MINER
No, no. Wait. They're bound to send a rescue team down for us. If you leave here you don't know what you're heading into.

MINER
I know that if we stay here we're done for.

MINER
We got to get moving now.

MINER
Somebody will come for us.

MINER
We got to get moving now! (*Emphasise*) Nobody's coming for us! If we stick together we'll be okay!

MINER
Stick together, we'll be okay? What do you think this is, the Boy Scouts? Well I'm going, I'm not staying here to fry! The updraught will pull the fire up here then it will be too late. I'm off!

MINER
Aye and it'll be drawing up the gas. The gas is creeping up here all the time, it's the pressure pulling it through, there's a hell of a draught, uffern, if it gets to these flames we'll all go up like a volcano!

MINER
Aye, if we don't suffocate first!

MINER
Shut up, will you! Try and think straight or we'll never get out of here.

MINER
Well let's get over to 142 Section like you said. (*He moves off but nobody else moves*). Come on then unless you want to die. (*Some men huddle together. One holds a lamp against the roof. It flares bright. He coughs.*)

MINER
Get down, the roof's full of gas!

MINER
Come on, come on, let's get down to that passage in 142 Section like you said!

MINER
But… (*He is dragged away holding a lump of rock*)

MINER
Look, we've got to get moving and bloody quick. (*He moves off but nobody follows.*) Come on then, unless you want to bloody die, well what's the matter with you, a minute ago you was in a big hurry, what we standing around for you said, let's get going you said. That's the way out, up there (*he points to the escape route*)

MINER
I'm not climbing up, it's 1000 feet to the surface!

MINER

We're staying here, stay with us.

MINER
You'll die if you stay here, come with us. If there's a way out we'll find it, let's get going. (*The escape route includes many exits and entrances*) I'm not climbing to the top, it's 1000 feet to the surface, we'll never make it. I'm heading for the cage. Come on, come on, what are you stopping for? The cage might still be working.

MINER
Wait, wait! (*He moves a broken prop that is blocking the way*)

MINER
Get a move on, we'll have the bloody lot down on top of us in a minute. What are you doing, having a tea break? Get moving, get moving.

MINER
There's a prop in the bloody way.

MINER
Let me through, out of the way, out of the way! (*He moves the prop.*) I'll go forward a bit.

MINER
What's it like along there?

MINER
I can't see. I need more light, bring your lamps up here, shine them along here.

MINER
What's it like? Can you see anything?

MINER
Can you see anything, Tommy, can you see anything? Why the bloody hell doesn't he answer? Tommy!

MINER
He's coming back.

MINER
What's the chances?

MINER
None, none. (*Despairingly*)

(*Exit left, exit right, enter trapdoor etcetera*)

MINER
I want to see, get out of the way! (*Moves into the hole to investigate*)

133

MINER
The floor's dropped 6 feet and the roof with it, will have to try somewhere else. We can find a way down Old 25 passageway.

(*Miner re-emerges, grumbles and waves his hand in defeat.*) (*They move off in different directions.*)

MINER
Keep low, there's gas along the roof. Keep going, keep going. Keep low, there's gas, don't stick your snouts up, one sniff of that and you're a goner!

MINER
Watch your head.

MINER
Aaargh!

MINER
What's the matter now. (*The miners stop and bunch up*)

MINER
It's going to go, it's going to go! (*Debris falls from the roof*) There's a cable in the way. Don't touch it, it's live.

MINER
Here, use this prop. (*He tries to push the sparking cable prop to one side*)

MINER
Well push it, push it, what you waiting for, Christmas? Get hold of the bloody thing! (*He pushes past the hesitant miner and pulls the cable to one side*)

MINER
I've found the passage but it's blocked. It's been walled up.

MINER
Walled up!

MINER
We can cut through it.

MINER
Cut through it, what with, we haven't got a pick.

MINER
There's got to be a pick around here somewhere! (*The miners scramble and find a pick and a crowbar. They cut a small hole.*)

MINER
Wait, wait, I'll have to test for gas! (*He holds his lamp against the hole. The lamp flame flares.*) Gas! (*They push the debris back into the hole*)

MINER
Gas! We won't last five seconds then! We'll have to go back.

OCKY
I thought you knew this section, you been working here two years you said. Did you have your eyes closed or what?

MINER
Calm down, Ocky, that sort of talk won't get us out of here!

OCKY
Won't get us out of here, won't get us out of here, we're going round in circles.

OVERMAN
We're going back!

OCKY
Why should we do what you say?

OVERMAN
Because I'm the Overman, now get going. Jacko, follow up at the rear.

(*Whispers at the back: Overman my arse, if he'd done his job properly in the first place we wouldn't be in this mess now!*)

OCKY
Well I (*emphasise*) want to know where I'm going, the fire's that way and it's catching up with us! We are heading straight into it!

OVERMAN
Well we'll try the conveyor road, with all the steelwork it might have held the roof and we'll be able to squeeze through somehow.

OCKY
Squeeze through somehow!

OVERMAN
Well have you got a better idea Ocky, or would you like to come along with us.

OCKY
To hell with that, I'm not going back down there, I'm off! (*Exits, running*)

MINER
We'll have to go on without Ocky. I'll go forward a bit and see what it's like. (*Exit, closely followed by another miner*)

MINER
There's an opening!

MINER
It's a dead end, I knew it, you can't go down there! We was cutting it out for a new ventilation shaft and then we was told to stop because we hit water coming in from an old working. Forget it!

MINER
It's worth a try!

MINER
Forget it! You'll hit solid rock, or water, it's probably filling up now.

MINER
That's what the management wanted you to think so they could get you off repair work and on to coal cutting, more money isn't it? There is a passage down here, I know it! We was working 50 yards over from here, I'm sure. (*The two miners move forward and find the opening*) I knew it, I knew it!

MINER (*Shouts*)
Any signs of life?

MINER
What's it like? Anything?

MINER (*Shouts*)
Any signs of life? Answer, will you! (*Hysterical shout*)

OVERMAN
Nothing... But no bodies, neither... So probably no gas. (*The men move along, Indian file, two or three of them shoulder to shoulder*)

MINER
Christ, this leads to the cage, I recognise it from two years ago, it's only three or 4 hundred yards from here.

OCKY (*returns*)
That's if it's still open!

MINER (*impatiently*)
Well we'll bloody well soon find out! Come on, you lead the way seeing as you know it.

MINER
There it is, there it is! (*They arrive at the Main Road junction and race along to the cage and bundle in and ring the bell for UP*) (*The roar of the fire increases*)

(*The escaped miners emerge from the winding house. They are surrounded by the waiting crowd. Blankets are put on their shoulders and mugs of tea are thrust into their hands.*) (*The moon and stars shine in the background.*)

MINERS
We're safe, we're safe.

ARTHUR
Yes but where is my brother, that's what I want to know? There's Dai Clogs from 29, he'll
know something. Dai, have you seen my brother?

DAI
No, I came up half an hour ago, you're the first I've seen come out of the Dennis.

ARTHUR
Do you know Albert Jones, he was on 29s tonight?

MINER
No.

ARTHUR
Do you know Albert Jones?

MINER
No.

MINER
Look, there's the Agent, ask him.

ARTHUR
What the bloody hell's happened, where is everybody else?

AGENT
There is no one else... yet.

ARTHUR
What do you mean, no one else, there's over two hundred men down there.

AGENT
I know, but –

AGENT'S ASSISTANT
Hold on a minute, we think there's a hundred men trapped, we'll be through to them in about
an hour's time, you must have seen the rescue party as you came up, we're doing everything
we can. You must go to the sick bay, there's a doctor there.

(*Mrs Jones pushes through the crowds, she carries Mr Jones's overcoat. She stares at each
of the six emerging miners who shakes his head as she approaches. Arthur and she move off
together. The crowd gathers around the miners, shouting questions as they exit and a
policeman intervenes.*)

POLICEMAN
Have faith Mrs... they'll bring them up, you'll see.

MRS JONES
I knew he shouldn't have gone tonight!

POLICEMAN
Go home and look after the children, they'll be worried by themselves.

(*The sound of machinery continues.*)

LIGHTS DOWN

A FEW DAYS LATER. THE BACK KITCHEN

MRS ROBERTS, NEIGHBOUR
Mrs Jones, please have a drink. (*She sets down a cup of tea before Mrs Jones.*) I'm sorry about Mr Jones and all the others, I lost my Jack, but you can't sit here all day, you're blue with cold. (*She feels her hand.*) It does no good.

MRS JONES
Mrs Roberts, is that you? (*Trance-like*) What am I doing sitting here? Albert will be up soon wanting his dinner and that fire needs making up, it's nearly dead! You know what he's like if there isn't a good blaze going. (*She pokes the fire furiously.*)

MRS ROBERTS (*the neighbour grabs hold of her.*)
Mrs Jones, he won't be getting up.

MRS JONES
Rake that fire will you, I must get the water boiling for his shave.

MRS ROBERTS
Mrs Jones, Albert won't be getting up. He's gone.

MRS JONES
Gone! Gone where? What are you talking about, gone!

MRS ROBERTS
He's gone, Mrs Jones, he's dead.

MRS JONES (*A long silence*)
No!

MRS ROBERTS
Yes.

MRS JONES
No, no. (*She sobs uncontrollably*)

MRS ROBERTS (*She slides a Bible across the table towards Mrs Jones*)
Maybe you could take comfort from the Bible, Mrs Jones.

MRS JONES (*She looks at it disconsolately. She pushes it back*)
No, not now, but, I will, in time.

MRS ROBERTS
Look…mmmm… I've bought some milk and bread. Have you eaten today? I don't suppose you got any money for food and things. (*She puts bread and milk from her bag on the table*)

MRS JONES
We're all right but he would have taken his wages down with him the same as everybody else.

ARTHUR (*Arthur enters*)
They've stopped searching. They are not sending any more rescue parties down, that last explosion on top was the last straw. He's dead you know, no chance… Three men in the rescue party killed. (*He shakes his head in disbelief*) (*He sets the paper package down on the table*) It's more herrings from those Scotch fishermen up in Aberdeen somewhere. Everybody gets a ration. I wish they'd send us a bit of salmon instead.

MRS JONES
Thank you Arthur, I'm going to the parlour to carry on packing. You stay here and have a cup of tea. (*She exits but turns*) He won't see our new house. (*disconsolately*)

MRS ROBERTS (*They wait until she disappears*)
Do you think they'll be able to get the men out… the bodies, I mean.

ARTHUR
Not unless they do it quick. In the next few weeks the floor will have gone up, (*He raises his arm*) and the roof will have come down. (*He lowers his arm.*) There won't be that much (*he shows his thumb and finger*) then it will be impossible, they'll be there forever.

(*Mrs Jones re-enters with Mr Jones's coat. She puts it into a case. She takes a photo off the shelf and places it on top of the folded coat.*)
(*Arthur is uneasy*)

ARTHUR
I'm off, I've got to sign on at the Labour. (*He embraces Mrs Jones and leaves. He exits the kitchen as there is a knock on the front door. Arthur re-enters.*) It was that tally man fellow, Jacobs, he said for me to give you this. (*Mrs Jones looks at the payment card. There was five shillings owing but it has PAID IN FULL stamped on it.*)

MRS JONES
Well ask him in.

ARTHUR
No, he's gone, he went straight away. I'm off too.

MRS JONES (*she reads the card out loud*)
Paid in full. We'll be able to buy you a new pair of shoes now. (*She looks at Ruth without feeling*)

A FEW DAYS LATER

ARTHUR *(Knock, knock, knock at the front door)*
I'll get it *(From the parlour)*

(Three well-dressed men enter with Arthur. They take their hats off)

SIR HENRY WALKER
Are you Mr Jones's widow?

MRS JONES
Yes, I was his wife…he was my husband.

SIR HENRY WALKER
I hope we haven't come at an inconvenient time, but it's about the accident.

MRS JONES
Oh, please let's go into the parlour.

SIR HENRY WALKER
No, no, this will be fine, thank you. Let me introduce myself. I am Sir Henry Walker and these gentlemen are my two assistants, Mr Edwards and Mr Smith. You may know that I am His Majesty's Inspector of Mines and as such it is my duty to inquire into the cause of the explosion at Gresford Colliery some weeks ago and to decide on the future of the colliery. We have already visited a number of families who have lost relatives and I know you are all very concerned about bringing um… rescuing the bodies… of your loved ones up from the pit and giving them a proper Christian burial.

MRS JONES
Oh yes. *(Mrs Jones slumps down into a chair)*

SIR HENRY WALKER
Well as I have said to all the other families that I have visited today, I'm afraid this will not be possible.

ARTHUR
Not possible!

SIR HENRY WALKER *(He takes a map from his briefcase and spreads it on the table)*
Look, this is where we believe the explosion took place and this is where we believe your husband and his colleagues are lying. As you can see, the way is blocked and the conditions are too dangerous for us to enter because of the fallen rock and of course the gas. We could bring some of them out but not all, by no means all, indeed we could bring out so few of the dead that we have decided they should all remain there. It will have to be their grave.

ARTHUR
But surely we could dig our way through once the fires have been damped down, it's been done before.

SIR HENRY WALKER
You just don't know how bad it is down there, I've seen it. The Company says it is too dangerous and I agree with them.

ARTHUR
They're afraid we'll find out the truth, more like, it wasn't too dangerous when they was making a profit.

SIR HENRY WALKER
It's too late to talk like that now, you should have spoken out six months ago.

ARTHUR
It's too late. It's too late. That's always the excuse, it's too late, until the next time, then it'll be too late again. Ha, I bet in a few months' time the pit will be open and they'll be cutting new faces right up close to the Dennis Section. It won't be too dangerous then, will it.

SIR HENRY WALKER
That's as maybe, but the Company has the right to keep the old section closed. (*He turns to Mrs Jones*) I'm sorry Mrs Jones but there is no more I can say... or do. All the bereaved are in the same situation. The section will have to remain closed... I'm afraid we will have to bid you good day Mrs Jones, we have many calls to make as I'm sure you will understand. (*He looks at Arthur*) Good day, Mr Jones. We'll see ourselves out. (*Exit*)(*Arthur accompanies them to the hallway, returns and stands in the kitchen doorway*)

ARTHUR
Well what do you make of that. A whitewash, a bloody whitewash, I knew it. I told you this would happen. The section will have to remain closed, closed my foot. They don't want us to get in there so we can see for ourselves what really happened.

MRS JONES
Do you think they will ever get the men out?

ARTHUR
No, I suppose not. (*Resigned*) The management will never allow two hundred and fifty bodies to be laid out on the yard at Gresford and the Government will never allow two hundred and fifty hearses to roll down Wrexham High Street for all the world to see. There would be a revolution. (*He moves over to the side*) Maybe one day we will learn the truth, but we'll all be dead and gone by then.

DAVY (*Davy enters carrying a laden box and places it on the table*)
I'm taking it over to the new house, is there anything else you want taking over?

MRS JONES
Yes, these, and be careful, I don't want you breaking them. (*Bang bang at the front door*) What now! See who it is, I don't want to speak to anybody. Tell them... Tell them I've gone up to the bonc. (*She continues packing boxes ready for the move to the new house*) (*Davy exits to the front door*) (*Voices at the front door*)

OFFICIALS
We are from the Claims Section of the Benefits Office. We would like to speak to Mrs Jones.

DAVY
She's not here, she's gone up to the bonc.

OFFICIAL
The where?

DAVY
The bonc… the bank!

OFFICIAL
The Bank! (*Astonished*) Oh I don't think you'll be needing our services. Good day!

MRS JONEs
(*Davy re-enters the kitchen*) What did they want?

DAVY
I don't know. They didn't say! I'm going now. (*Davy exits with box*)

LIGHTS DOWN

Weeks later, after leaving the old house.

Mrs Jones enters the darkened kitchen of the old house. The sound of scraping above, she looks up. A shaft of sunlight penetrates the gloom and strikes her face, creating an angel -like glow around her head. Some debris falls on her from above. It's a demolition worker removing slates from the roof. A worker enters through the door, allowing sunlight to enter, lightening the room. We now see floor planks from the bedroom floor scattered about and also piled neatly ready for transportation. Against the window lean a number of planks blocking out the sunlight.

BUILDER
Wait a minute Jack, there's a woman down here!
You shouldn't be here walking around at this time of night. You were lucky you didn't have your head knocked off, were clocking off in a few minutes… Didn't you see the warning outside?

MRS JONES
No. No.

BUILDER
What are you doing here anyway?

MRS JONES
I used to live here.

BUILDER
Oh, come to see it for old time sake, eh, before it's all gone!

MRS JONES
Well, not quite. Gone, you say?

142

BUILDER
Most of the roof and the slates will be gone by tomorrow, and all the stone in a few days, some contractors bought all this row, there'll be nothing here by next week. Well I'm sorry but you'll have to shift pretty smart, we're ready to go home and the foreman will be…

MRS JONES
Yes, I understand, sorry. Thanks. (*Exit*)

BUILDER
She's gone, you can carry on now. What the hell she wanted to come back here for I don't know. You'd have thought she'd be (*The demolition continues. Debris falls from the roof*) glad to see the back of this place. Bloody hell, wait till I'm out of the door! (*Exit*)

LIGHTS DOWN

(*Enter Davy. He places an object, the silver box in the ground where the hedgehog is buried. He looks about him. He scrapes the soil back over it*) (*Exit*)

(*Curtains or lights open on the kitchen of the old house in darkness*)

(*Mrs Jones enters alone. She shines a torch, she walks carefully over to the wall cupboard and opens a door. She retrieves an object from it, looks at it and places it in her pocket after pressing it to her chest*) (*enter Ruth followed by Davy*)

RUTH
Mama, Mama! (*Running*)

MRS JONES
I told you to stay outside!

RUTH
I was afraid Mama, it's dark!

MRS JONES (*to Davy*)
And where have you been, I've been waiting for you.

DAVY
I saw a man from work so I stopped to talk to him.

MRS JONES
Well keep hold of her!

(*The room brightens as the cloud separates and the moon can be seen through the open roof. Moonlight penetrates the darkness*)

MRS JONES
Oh! Look, Shino, we can see the moon!

(More clouds separate) *(Moonlight shines on both of them, halo-like)*

RUTH
And the stars!

(Lights down except for the moon and stars)

MUSIC – GRESFORD: The Miner's Hymn: Robert Saint

THE END

Printed in Great Britain
by Amazon

47423876R00086